At HOME

CARLY MARIE

CONTENTS

Editing Services: Susie Selva

Cover By: FuriousFotog

CHAPTER 1

DEREK

"Hey, Derek, we're going to the bar. You coming?" Harrison called to me, as I headed to the dressing room at the back of the arena.

We were the founding members of the country music band, Hometown. Harrison was the bass guitarist and had grown up with me in Oklahoma. I was lead vocals for the band and played acoustic guitar as well.

I nodded. "Give me twenty." An evening at the bar would be just what my frazzled nerves needed, but first, I needed a shower. My hair was soaked with sweat and my black t-shirt clung to my body. Another two-hour set was in the books and we were almost halfway through our first headlining tour.

Harrison and I had spent a few years playing small bars for a little pocket change while we were in college. We had never intended to become famous or to end up with a number one album. But that is exactly what happened. We were approached by a talent scout after playing at a honky-tonk in Tulsa. In the blink of an eye, our little side gig turned into our livelihoods.

Within a few months of that chance encounter, we were in a studio in Nashville recording our first album. Our current headlining tour followed a six-month tour opening for one of the hottest country artists in the nation.

Since playing that bar in Tulsa, I had gone from Derek Edward Scott, a twenty-two year old ranch hand on my family's ranch, college student, and struggling artist and songwriter, to twenty-four year old Derek Edwards. Derek Edwards was a country music sensation, playing sold-out arenas, various music awards shows, and oh yeah, a Grammy award-winning artist.

How the fuck did that *happen?*

Our first single had shot straight to the top of the charts and our lives had been an insane roller coaster ride ever since.

There was a part of me that missed just being a college student and working on my parents' ranch in the summers. As quickly as that thought entered my mind, it was joined by memories of the uncomfortable Christmas I spent with my family three weeks earlier. I'd been dragged to church to listen to the pastor drone on about Jesus, Mary, and Joseph. I'd heard the same sermon so often I could practically recite it by heart.

What I hadn't expected was the extra fifteen minutes of the pastor lecturing the entire congregation about how the "gay agenda" was threatening Christianity and the sanctity of this holy time. I'd sat in the pew with my mouth hanging open, wondering how the gays were killing Christmas.

Okay, so, maybe being a chart-topping country artist who only had time to go home for a couple of days every four or five months wasn't so bad after all.

I showered as quickly as I could and headed to find Harrison and whoever else was going to join us at the bar. We had just finished playing in Nashville which proved to be every bit as insane as we expected. We knew we couldn't go to a bar anywhere in the city because we'd be mobbed by fans. Instead, Harrison was on his phone searching for bars off the beaten path to hopefully give us a bit of anonymity and allow us some much needed time to relax.

"Where're we going?" I questioned, as I pulled on a black and white plaid button-up over a white undershirt. I rolled the sleeves halfway up my forearms and grabbed an old college ball cap before being satisfied with my appearance.

Harrison grinned. "Franklin. It's about thirty minutes from here, kinda the middle of nowhere."

Gina, one of our backup singers, turned vital member of the band, clapped happily. "Night out!" She was a petite little thing, topping the scale at maybe one hundred and ten pounds soaking wet and was no more than five-foot-three. Her hair was purple, at least that week, by the next week it would likely be a different color.

The first few weeks of the tour, Gina had flirted with me almost constantly, but after pulling her aside one night and telling her I wasn't interested in her, or any woman, she backed off and became a friend and fierce ally.

I'd been out in college and our management team had been quick to separate Derek Scott and Derek Edwards. The thought was if they could bury the existence of Derek Scott, an out gay man, then there wouldn't be much dirt on me. I hadn't been all that comfortable with the idea at first. I'd just gotten comfortable enough with my sexuality to come out to friends. The last thing I wanted to do was go back into the closet. A number of worst case scenarios had been thrown my way before I finally agreed to the name change.

It had been over a year and there didn't seem to be many, if any, people who had figured out we were the same person. The media finding out had quickly become my biggest fear. Country music wasn't ready for a gay musician, yet.

I had reluctantly agreed to go back into the closet with the understanding I would be able to tell the band. When we signed the contract, I didn't want my personal life to be public knowledge anyway. I'd always been a private person and I preferred to keep it that way. In private though, I didn't want to hide my sexuality. I needed the band to know I was gay because it was a part of who I was. Unfortunately, the fear management had ingrained in me made it hard to be open, even with the band. It had taken me months to come out to everyone on the tour with us. We were a tight knit group and so far nothing about my sexuality had been leaked online or to the media.

I was happy to keep it that way.

Gina, Harrison, and I were joined by Clayton, Vance, and Neil, all backup musicians hired by the label, but we had quickly become friends. We climbed into a black SUV and Harrison leaned forward to input the address into the driver's phone. "Please, keep us under the radar. We just need a night out," he said to the man.

The driver nodded and began to follow the directions on his phone while we laughed and chatted in the back. The farther from Nashville we got, the more I was able to relax. It had been too long since I was Derek Scott and I missed going out with friends. The last eighteen months had been a whirlwind and it was nice to be able to take a step back.

"We've just snuck out," I said with a laugh. "Sneaking out of Nashville is a lot harder than it was to sneak out of our houses growing up."

Harrison laughed too. "Remember that night in high school when we snuck out of your house to go to the movies with our girlfriends and your dad was sitting on the front porch as we rounded the house?"

We dove into a row of bushes on the side of the drive-way, both forgetting they were my mom's roses. By the time we got ourselves untangled from the bushes, we were scratched and our clothes were torn from the thorns. Thankfully, we were able to keep our pained screams muffled and got away before my dad found us.

Gina shot me a mischievous grin. "Girlfriend?"

"You didn't grow up in an Evangelical household. I faked it until I was in college. I didn't come out to my immediate family until just before the tour started. I'm still not out to our fans. At this rate, we'll be retired before I find a guy to be with."

I was on track for the longest dry spell ever.

Harrison bumped me with his shoulder. "There's no reason that has to be the case. You've made enough money on this tour to never need to go back to Oklahoma again. Be happy for once."

I rolled my eyes at him as the SUV pulled into the parking lot of a small bar in the middle of a tiny town. "Good job, Harrison, you found a bar off the beaten path!" Clayton said, his voice laced with sarcasm. There were two SUVs with Sheriff Department markings in the lot and maybe ten other cars and trucks. We piled out of the back and headed into the bar.

There was a slight lull in conversations as the six of us walked in the front door of Steve's Tavern. The most generic bar name in the most generic looking place ever. *Thank you Harrison!* I had to refrain from turning and hugging him in the middle of the bar.

Most of the bar's occupants allowed their eyes to sweep over the five men in our group when we first entered. It was clear this was a local bar and outsiders were uncommon. And none of us were small guys, Neil was the shortest and slightest built of all of us, but even he was almost six feet tall and solid muscle. Once they took us in, they all seemed to notice Gina standing behind us and more than one set of male eyes appraised her. I pulled my ball cap down farther to avoid recognition.

"I'm here to have fun," Gina whispered, "and so help

me, if any of you pull the big brother card and gets in the way, I'm going to have your balls."

We all laughed and headed directly to the bar. Gina already had a man approaching her, offering to buy her a drink, so I grabbed a beer with the other guys and we headed to a table in the corner.

An hour later, I excused myself to use the restroom in the back of the bar. On my way out, I was distracted by a text from my brother and I ran face first into a solid wall of muscle, knocking my ball cap to the ground. My six-foot frame was nothing compared to the tall, dark, and handsome man standing in front of me wearing a dark green uniform shirt that read "Sheriff Westfield." His sleeves were rolled up over his elbows and his exposed arms were thick with sinewy muscles that moved hypnotically. He put his hands on my shoulders to steady me as I took a few steps back. I felt electricity zing through the spots where our bodies touched. "Sorry," I muttered, as I bent to pick my ball cap up off the ground and slid my phone into my pocket. My brother could wait.

I had a hard time looking the gorgeous man in his piercing green eyes.

"No problem," the guy, Sheriff Westfield I presumed, said in a deep voice with a slight tip of his own hat.

He walked into the bathroom and I had to pull myself together, quick. "*Not now, Derek,*" I scolded myself. "*This is not the time, or the place. Jesus fucking Christ, you are on tour.*"

My growing arousal was going to be a problem, so I started thinking of mathematical equations, the next tour stop, anything to make me stop thinking about the Adonis who had just walked into the bathroom. I finally pulled my phone out of my pocket again, thinking maybe returning my brother's text would distract me enough my cock would stand down, and I could go back to my friends without a hard-on in my jeans.

"Can't seem to get away from you," a deep voice said from in front of me, causing me to jump slightly.

So much for distraction.

CHAPTER 2

COLT

LAUGHING NERVOUSLY, THE MAN I HAD BEEN watching since he walked into the bar responded, "Yeah, I guess not. Small bar and all."

"I'm Colt," I introduced myself, extending my hand.

"Derek," he replied tentatively. His blue eyes watched my face closely as if he was waiting for me to say something. His lower lip was red, swollen from where he had been chewing on it while staring at his phone.

"Nice to meet you, Derek. Can I buy you a drink?"

Why was I offering to buy this guy a drink?

I had originally planned on leaving after hitting the bathroom, but his adorably flushed cheeks and the bashful grin he was giving me had all my dominant instincts on full alert.

Judging by the thorough once over he'd given me when we bumped into each other, I was pretty sure the interest was not one sided. Appearance wise, he was just my type; tall and muscular without being taller than me or looking

9

like a gym rat. His shaggy blonde hair and big, blue, puppy-dog eyes gave him a younger, more innocent appearance. He was younger than me for sure, but not jail-bait. If I had to guess, I'd say he was in his mid-twenties. That would make him a full ten years younger than I was, give or take.

And if that thought didn't have my inner Daddy Dom waking up...

We walked up to the bar together and I looked over at him. "What would you like?"

He seemed startled I had asked him and he blinked a few times. "Oh, um, an IPA?" I didn't know if he had meant it to be a question, but the way he was looking at me for approval was making my dick stir in my jeans.

I nodded and looked at the bartender. "Two IPAs. Do you have a preference?" I asked him.

"Whatever's on tap, please," he said to the guy behind the counter.

I nodded. "Sounds good to me."

We didn't talk while our drinks were being poured, though the quiet wasn't uncomfortable. I slid the bartender some money for the drinks and a few dollars tip then turned my attention back to Derek. I tilted my head toward the opposite corner of the bar, away from the music and the corner where his friends were. I thought we could talk more easily away from those distractions.

He took a long drink of his beer and sighed. It was a soft noise I hadn't expected from him. We had barely spent ten minutes in each other's company, but there was some-thing about Derek that was appealing to me on a primal level. I was already having to discreetly adjust myself before we'd even had a chance to talk.

"This is really good," he said, as he set the glass down. "Thank you for buying."

"Of course. So, Derek, what brings you to Steve's tonight?"

He shrugged like he was unsure what to say. "Just needed a night to relax. Our schedule doesn't allow us time to get out much."

I glanced over at the group he had arrived with, "What is it that keeps you all so busy?"

Derek fiddled with the glass like he was trying to figure out how to answer me. He finally looked up and smiled. "We're in showbusiness."

That explained why they weren't able to get out much in the evening. If they were a road crew for a band, they would probably be working almost every night. Given how grueling that life was, I would expect they probably slept the few nights they had off.

"You're in law enforcement?" Derek questioned, before I could think much more about it.

I nodded. "I'm the sheriff of an area about a half an hour from here. I met a friend tonight to discuss a case we've been working on involving both our jurisdictions."

Derek's eyes twinkled. "If you do your job half as well as you wear that uniform, I bet you're amazing."

I choked on my beer and Derek's cheeks turned red. "Oh my god, I have no idea where that came from!" he gasped, his hand covering his mouth in surprise.

I held up a finger for him to give me a minute. I had to

take a few deep breaths before I could talk again, and I was sure my face was red from inhaling the beer. "It's okay. I'll gladly take the compliment." *Especially from a hot young guy like him.* At least that confirmed any lingering questions I had about his sexuality. "Thanks, you're cute, too."

I was rewarded with another blush and another dip of his head. I wished he would take his hat off so I could see more of his face. The little glimpses I was seeing were driving me wild.

Derek's cheeks heated, but he managed to laugh. "Thank you, Sheriff."

"Where are you from?" I asked, curious about his unfamiliar accent. It was faint, but it was there.

"Oklahoma. Though, I think I may be looking at moving to this area. My job seems to find me around here pretty often."

I nodded like it made perfect sense. If he did work for a country musician, he would probably be in Nashville frequently.

"Do you want another beer?" I asked, when his was gone.

He shook his head, "No, I shouldn't drink any more. I had a few when we first got here and I have to work tomorrow."

I appreciated a man who knew his limits and when to say enough was enough. "Good boy," I said, without thought.

Shit, that was going to kill any chance I had with Derek. I had never met a man outside of a fetish club that liked to be called "boy."

It took an ex telling me he didn't want to be my submissive and he wasn't into that "kinky shit" during a fight before I realized I was a Dom. I had never thought of it that way before because I didn't *have* to be in control all the time, and I wasn't a strict top. I was verse and, while I like to take control in the bedroom sometimes, I was happy with a fairly even give and take most of the time. Given the right partner, I liked bottoming, especially when I could find someone who was able to tap into the part of me that loved things a little rough. There was something satisfying about feeling it the next day I occasionally craved, but most men I had been with were too intimidated by my size to try.

In the five years since I discovered that part of me, I'd played with a wide variety of subs. For the first few years, I mistakenly thought there was only one way to be a Dom. I was able to be a firm-handed, authoritative Dom for a submissive who craved harsh punishments, but I never found the pleasure I thought I should with the whips, paddles, and floggers.

A few years later, I was at a fetish club and was approached by a bouncy little guy wearing a thick diaper and a light blue leather harness with a pacifier clipped to it who asked me if I wanted to play. That night had been eye opening for me. He had spent most of the time sitting in my lap while I talked with a few friends. When he began humping into my hand that had absently found the front of his diaper and his eager hard-on, I'd told him to stop. To his credit, he tried a number of times before I finally told him if he continued I was going to have to put him over my knee. Needless to say, he ended up over my knee, his diapered ass sticking up while I spanked him. The loud thuds of my hand hitting the thick diaper and him humping my leg for all he had was everything I had been craving. After finally giving him permission to cum he layed curled up in my arms, nursing his pacifier until it was time to leave.

I went home and spent the next week researching everything I could about age play and the domination and power exchange surrounding it. That was when I learned that I was, at heart, a Daddy Dom, but finding a boy in the lifestyle had been a lot harder.

To my surprise, Derek's breath caught in his throat and he stopped playing with his empty glass. His eyes widened and he shifted slightly in his seat. *There is no way I'm going to be this lucky, I can't even find a boy to play with at a fetish club most of the time.* He looked at me and gave me a sweet smile. "Thank you." It felt like he wanted to say something else, but he stopped himself.

I leaned over and whispered low, "Do you like being a good boy?"

Derek's eyes fluttered closed and his breathing turned ragged. *Had I really just rattled him with that one question?* Fuck, I was going to be in trouble with this guy.

"Derek?" I asked.

He blinked up at me. "Oh, um, I-yes," he stammered, as color flared in his cheeks and down his neck.

Fuck, all the dirty images running through my head were going to fry *my* brain. I needed to get myself under control quickly. I wasn't twenty anymore, my recovery period was longer than it once was. I couldn't portray a confident Dom if I came in my pants just from Derek's admission.

Derek leaned back in his chair and casually spread his legs apart slightly. My eyes fell to his crotch where I could see the outline of his full cock through his jeans. "I've got a hotel in the Nashville area, would you want to come back with me?" He bit his lower lip and stared up at me with those beautiful puppy-dog eyes.

He was an intoxicating mess of contradictions—strong and assertive, asking me to go to his hotel one second, the next second, shy and hesitant while he worried his lip waiting for my answer.

"That sounds like a good idea. Are you safe to drive?" I asked him. His eyes had appeared a little glassy the last few minutes. He wasn't drunk, but he had definitely had a few beers.

Derek shook his head. "I didn't drive. One of the drivers brought us."

"Would you like me to take you back to your hotel?"

Derek's eyes lit up. "I'd love a ride. They don't look like they're ready to leave yet," he noted while looking over at his friends. "It wouldn't be right for me to leave them stranded," his voice sounded serious, but the twinkle in his eyes said he knew exactly what he was doing.

He grabbed his phone and tapped out a quick message to his group of friends. "Okay, they know I'm heading back to the hotel," he said to me.

CHAPTER 3

DEREK

By the time we arrived in Nashville, I didn't know if I could make it to my hotel room without cumming. We had spent the drive teasing each other with touches through our clothes. Colt had started by resting his large hand on my knee, but it gradually moved up my thigh. Each time I squirmed, he would inch it up. By the time I saw the highway sign for the hotel, his hand was resting inches from my crotch and I was about to start whimpering.

Of course, I wasn't innocent either. While I knew better than to distract someone while they were driving, especially if that person had the ability to arrest me, I decided stop lights were fair game. Each time we hit a red light, I would touch him—his inner thigh, the pulsepoint on his neck, his ear. The last light we hit, I ran my fingernail over one of his nipples. Colt dragged in a ragged breath at the touch, and I filed the information away for later. Colt had just enough of a no-nonsense vibe about him that I didn't want to push him too far. I wasn't looking for a punishment that night. I needed my ass filled and judging by the bulge in his dark wash jeans, he was well equipped to handle the job.

What I hadn't told Colt was the last time I hooked up with a guy was months before the tour started. With the stress of being found out by the paparazzi, I'd been on my best behavior. Tonight, though, I didn't really care if someone saw us entering the hotel together, I just wanted him inside me as soon as possible.

I mentally added uniform fetish to my list of possible kinks.

"Go toward the back," I instructed as we pulled into the hotel parking lot. Sure, we could have parked in the front and used the main entrance. But if we used the main entrance, we risked being seen by fans. I didn't think my dick could wait another minute to have Colt in my room. There was a chance I would explode if we weren't alone together soon.

The only reason I was comfortable with this in the first place was that Colt clearly had no clue who I was. To him, I wasn't a chart topping country musician, I was just another guy in town on business. It had been far too long since I had felt like a normal person. A bunch of people screaming my name when they saw me would definitely give me away. *No,* I was not going to risk what might be my one chance to hook up with someone during this tour, especially someone who had no clue who Derek Edwards was.

Colt looked at me in confusion. "The back of the hotel?"

"Private entrance. Perk of the job," I joked and tried a casual smile.

Colt seemed to take it in stride and pulled the SUV to the back of the lot. Even if someone found out where the band was staying, a sheriff's SUV pulling behind the building after midnight was not going to raise suspicion. He pulled into a spot under a light and killed the engine.

When Colt spoke, his voice was low and sexy. "You were a very good boy on the way here. You didn't distract me when I was driving, and you didn't beg me for anything." Damn he was good; was it possible he didn't know he was turning my brain to mush?

"Thank you..." What did I say after that? Sir? Daddy?

Fuck, the thought of calling Colt "Daddy" was doing all sorts of things to my insides. I could definitely put a big check mark beside Daddy kink on my rapidly growing mental list.

I had known from early on I liked to top sometimes, but I *loved* to bottom. That wasn't hard to figure out for a teenager with access to the internet and a few sex toys. What was more difficult to understand was the fact that sometimes, I liked to give up control. I didn't want to think or make decisions. I didn't consider myself a true submissive, though. I didn't need to give up control all the time, and I had learned most people took their submission further than I did. I wasn't looking to be whipped or flogged. I didn't want to be on my knees for a master. Sometimes, I just wanted to curl up with a strong man and be held and feel loved.

A few years earlier, I had come across Daddy kink on a blog and I knew I wanted to try it. A Daddy could decide when I could cum and what I did in the bedroom, but he would also be there for me when I needed affection and attention more than sex. I never found a guy who was a Daddy Dom before my career took off. Once I found myself in Nashville with a band and a tour schedule, I knew finding someone to roleplay that particular fantasy with would be much more difficult. I reluctantly filed the fantasy away in the, "maybe someday" box.

Having Colt call me a *good boy* and praising me for my behavior was bringing the fantasy crashing back to the forefront of my mind.

Would he flip out if I called him Daddy? The thought was enough to drive me crazy. We had only just met and I was trying to jump into calling him Daddy. I needed something to distract me.

Getting to the room. That would distract me, hopefully. At least I had to pay attention to what floor I was going to and what room number was on my keycard.

Colt chuckled beside me and I snapped my head to look at him. His eyebrows were raised as he looked at me expectantly. I had clearly missed something. "I'm sorry, did you say something?" I hoped my voice sounded calmer than my brain felt.

"I asked if my good boy was ready to go to the room for a reward."

My mouth went dry and my brain shut off again. I finally managed a nod and squeaked out an answer. "Yes...

sir?" That was not what I wanted to call him but it was what had come out.

He gave me a brief nod. "That will do, for now. Wait there, I'll get your door for you." Colt's voice left no room to question him, so I sat patiently as he got out of the car and came around to my side.

When he opened my door, I realized I was still buckled. I apparently couldn't get my brain to function enough to realize the first step of getting *out* of the car was to unfasten the seat belt. Colt simply smiled and leaned over me to unlatch the buckle like it was the most natural thing in the world. He stepped aside to give me plenty of space to exit.

Once freed from the SUV, I stood dumbly, seemingly unable to move as Colt shut the door and pushed the button on the keyfob to lock it. He was patient, if not a little amused, as we made our way to the back door, my unsteady legs slowing us down.

I felt his hand at the small of my back directing me, and I wondered if part of it wasn't him making sure I was close enough that he could catch me if my legs gave out on me completely. I didn't think I'd ever been as aroused as I was and I was glad to have Colt's hand guiding me, even if it wasn't helping me focus.

The cold January air helped my brain come back online, and by the time we reached the door I was feeling much steadier. I pulled the keycard out and scanned it on the pad near the back door that opened up to a dimly lit hallway and a single elevator. I led us to the elevator and pressed the up button. The doors opened immediately and we stepped in.

Colt stood closer than was strictly necessary, but I liked the feel of him close to me. I looked up and caught a glimpse of the camera in the corner and I knew I was going to have to keep my hands off him until we got into the room. That was going to be harder than I cared to think about.

I pressed the number for the sixth floor and bounced impatiently on the balls of my feet, wanting the elevator to go faster.

"Patience," Colt whispered in my ear. "It will be well worth the wait once we get to your room."

I may have whimpered—again.

As soon as the elevator doors opened enough for me to squeeze out, I was pushing my way through and looking for my room. I'd been here when we got to Nashville—long enough to drop off a few bags and catch a short nap before the show—so I knew the bank of rooms the band had were down the private hallway to my left. There was no real reason for guests to be down this way since the main elevator was around the corner and at the other end of the hall.

I tried not to look too anxious as I walked quickly toward the door marked 647. Scanning the keycard on the door, I let out a relieved sigh when it gave an approving *beep* and the lock clicked open.

CHAPTER 4

COLT

THE ROOM WAS DARK WHEN THE DOOR SHUT, BUT I didn't care, I needed my lips on Derek like I needed air in my lungs. He'd been making beautifully needy sounds the entire way to the hotel and the tentative touches he had peppered me with every time we stopped had my arousal at a record high.

I spun Derek around, backed him against the closed door knocking his hat to the floor, and kissed him hard on the mouth. This was not a tentative, exploratory, first kiss. This was a dominating, claiming kiss. I wanted him to know that, for tonight, he was mine.

Derek whimpered against my lips, opening his mouth wider to allow me full access. I swiped my tongue against his and I could feel when he completely surrendered control to me. His tongue didn't battle mine, he just willingly took everything I gave him.

I felt his arm move behind me. First, I heard the privacy lock click into place on the door, then the room behind me lit up. Without the harsh neon from the signs behind the bar or the shadows cast by his ball cap, I could finally see Derek's crystal blue eyes. They were unlike any color I'd ever seen before, reminding me of bright blue ocean water. His pupils were wide from the dim lighting and lust coursing through him, and I could only see a small ring of blue, but it was the most stunning blue I had ever seen.

I reached between us and palmed his erection through his tight jeans and he moaned. "Please," he whimpered.

"Please, what?" I knew he wanted more, but I had no idea where he wanted this to go.

"Please, more. I-I want to taste you," he managed to get out before moaning into my kiss again.

I took his hand and turned around to look at the room for the first time. I was shocked at how big it was. It was more like an upscale apartment than a hotel room. *Who the hell did he work for?* We were standing in a short entrance hallway that opened up to a spacious living area with a large couch positioned across from an electric fireplace and large TV. Beyond the living area was a small kitchen and breakfast area with sliding doors opening onto a small balcony.

Derek was chewing his lip anxiously as we walked into the living area. I couldn't decide if he was worried about what came next or what I thought of the room. Aside from the momentary shock at the sight, I didn't care what the room looked like. All I cared about was the gorgeous man in front of me.

I had a choice to make, but I had to make it quickly.

My gut said Derek was silently begging for me to take the lead and direct him. I just didn't know if it would scare him away if I went with it.

"Derek," I said, my voice firm and deep. When his eyes flickered up to mine I knew I had his attention. "You've been such a good boy for me tonight, can you answer a question for me honestly?"

His head bobbed up and down so fast I worried he would give himself whiplash. "Do you want me to tell you what to do tonight?" I would have preferred to simply ask, *Do you want Daddy to take control?* But I was afraid that would have been too much for him.

Derek's mouth opened and closed a few times while he looked for the right words. "Yes. Yes, please. I-I need that right now." It was more than I had expected him to say, but I was incredibly pleased by his answer.

His response also let me know he wanted the domination. We hadn't talked about limits or safewords and with him already needy, I wasn't going to push too far. Firm guidance, clear instructions, and a lot of praise for good listening shouldn't be too much for him.

My voice settled into the deep, steady, baritone that came out when my Dom side came out to play. "Alright, we're going to go to the living room and I'm going to give you a reward for being good and answering my question. I bet you want to touch me right now."

Derek nodded and whimpered as he reached down to adjust himself.

"Oh no, that is mine tonight, you don't get to touch that."

Derek fisted his hands at his sides and waited for the next instruction. I wondered if I should help him out of his tight jeans before we started, but dismissed the idea. The tight material pushing against him uncomfortably would, hopefully, ground him just enough that he wouldn't fall completely into subspace. I wished I could watch him drop that far, but we only had one night, and we hadn't talked about anything like that. It would be irresponsible of me to take him there without ever talking about it first or knowing what he needed afterward.

I walked over to the couch, but before I sat down I looked at the beautiful man standing where I left him, waiting so patiently for his instructions. "Come over here, Derek, I want you right in front of me."

I unbuttoned my uniform pants and slowly slid the zipper down. Derek watched my hands intently, his mouth parted. His eyes widened as my red boxer briefs came into view. Working the pants down my thighs, he got the first view of my erection pressing hard against my underwear. I could feel where precum had already dampened the fabric.

"Can I taste?" he questioned, looking up at me through thick lashes. The question caused my dick to jump.

"You may. Thank you for remembering your manners. I like when boys are so polite." Derek glowed and let out a soft moan at the praise. I loved how responsive he was, and it made me want to find everything that made him make those sounds.

I pulled my jeans off and ignored my own clumsy movements. Derek had me so turned on that even I was fumbling. I pulled my boxers down at the same time Derek sunk to his knees in front of me exhibiting far more grace than I could ever have managed.

His tongue darted out and he lapped the precum off my slit. He looked up at me through his lashes, waiting for permission to explore further. "Go ahead," I said, running my hand through his thick blonde hair. It was impossible to keep my hands out of his curls while he was on his knees in front of me.

Derek didn't hesitate to open wide and swallow me down. I gasped as the head of my cock touched the back of his throat. He had no gag reflex and was proud to show it off. His head bobbed slightly up and down, wet hot heat engulfing every part of my dick and dragging deep guttural sounds from me. Every sound I made caused Derek to double his efforts—faster, tighter, impossibly deeper.

Oh shit, I wasn't going to last long. I gripped his hair in both hands, willing myself not to thrust into his mouth. When his hands came around to grip each of my ass cheeks, his fingers slightly skimming my crease, I lost my will to hold back my orgasm.

"Derek, I'm going to cum," I warned him. If he didn't want me cumming down his throat, he was going to need to back off quickly.

The warning only spurred him on. He pulled back so only half of my dick was in his mouth, took a deep breath, and used my ass cheeks to pull me into his mouth even deeper than I had been before. He hollowed his cheeks, buried his nose in the well-trimmed hair above my dick, and swallowed. I felt his throat contract around me and then he hummed. The vibrations shot through my entire body, pulling my orgasm out of me in a way I had never felt before.

I shot volley after volley of cum down Derek's throat and he swallowed everything eagerly, not pulling back until I had been wrung completely dry. My heart was hammering so hard I was pretty sure it was visible through my shirt.

He sat back on his heels and looked up at me. "I love doing that."

I bent down close to Derek and put my index finger under his chin, drawing his lips to mine. "You don't say?" I asked before my lips landed on his. I could still taste my release in his mouth and I let the kiss linger a moment longer.

When we parted, Derek nodded his head. "I love giving blowjobs, but I haven't had a lot of chances to. The last few guys I've been with haven't been all that into it for some reason. But it's one of my favorite ways to pleasure a guy."

"Fuck," I moaned as my dick twitched. Derek leaned forward and nuzzled the tender skin where my groin met my thigh and just like that, I could feel blood beginning to flow back into my cock. There was something about Derek my body couldn't seem to get enough of.

I guided Derek to his feet and turned my attention to him. "You were so good, it's my turn to give *you* a reward." Derek's cock was long and thick from what I could tell through his jeans. My fingers went to the button of his fly and I flicked it open. As I slid the zipper down, a tiny pair of electric blue briefs greeted me. They were barely big enough to contain the erection that was pushing up and to the left, the tip almost peeking out of the top of the waistband.

He was so turned on the waistband was wet with precum. My hand grazed his dick as I freed it from his briefs, and his entire body shuddered at the touch. After guiding his legs from his pants and underwear, I finally got my first unobstructed view of his cock. It was thick, but perfectly proportioned to his body. He wasn't too long, he wasn't too thick. I could easily fit him in my mouth, though I wouldn't be able to swallow him down like he could me. Unfortunately, my gag reflex was well-intact.

We both still had our shirts on and I wanted to see his bare chest. "Take your shirt off for me." I stepped back from him just enough to give us both room to remove our shirts. I don't think I had ever managed to get the buttons of my shirt undone so quickly in all my life.

Derek was already pulling his t-shirt over his head when I finally had my uniform shirt on the couch behind me. I watched as he finished pulling his shirt over his head, exposing the deep grooves of his defined abs. His toned stomach and pecs were just as perfect as the rest of his body.

I pulled my t-shirt off and tossed it on the couch so I could get my hands on his smooth chest. Derek had very little hair anywhere on his body which turned me on even more. His smooth creamy skin wasn't obscured, allowing me to truly appreciate his toned physique.

I reached out and ran the pad of my thumb over his nipple. His head fell back and he leaned into the touch.

"Please, please, fuck me," he begged as he wrapped his large hand around his cock and began to stroke himself slowly.

"No, baby, that's mine to play with tonight, not yours. Remember?" I brushed his hand to the side.

Derek nodded. "I remember," he whispered, a beautiful pink blush creeping up his cheeks.

"Good. Now, do you have supplies here?" I asked him. There was a condom and lube in my wallet, but I was hoping he at least had a full bottle of lube somewhere in the room.

"Bathroom counter, in the black bag."

I kissed his forehead. "I'll be right back. I want you on your hands and knees in front of the fireplace when I get back."

I rushed into the bathroom, momentarily taken aback by how large it was, but quickly remembered the gorgeous man waiting for me in the living room. I found his toiletry bag on the counter and grabbed the bottle of lube and a few condoms from inside. I also swiped two towels from the towel bar. The hotel carpet, no matter how nice, would not be comfortable on his knees.

When I returned to the living room, Derek was exactly where I told him to be. His perfectly round ass was beautifully on display as he rested forward on his chest and forearms, his pink pucker visible between his ample cheeks. "Fuck," I gasped, unable to formulate a coherent thought..

"Here, this will be more comfortable on your knees than the carpet," I suggested as I shook the towels out.

Derek looked at me over his shoulder with one

eyebrow raised high. "You think I care about my knees right now? All I care about is your dick in my ass." But he humored me and moved onto the towel. "Okay, knees are good. Dick, ass, now."

I barked out a laugh. "Bossy bottom." Apparently, my time in the bathroom had been just enough for him to regain his senses, and now all he wanted was to get fucked.

"You know it. Now please, hurry. I don't need a lot of prep," he moaned as my finger traced his crease. "A quick finger or two, I like the burn."

Fuck.

I was already well on my way to hard again. My recovery time hadn't been this quick since my teen years.

Despite Derek's pleas, I was going to take my time. I knelt behind him, my hands kneading the firm globes of his ass as I worked my thumbs closer to his crease. Derek's breath caught as my thumb finally grazed over his rim.

I had to force myself to still my hand as he pushed his ass back, begging for me to enter him. He let out a frustrated groan as my thumb moved from his hole and I waited.

"Patience," I whispered as his body stilled. He vibrated with need as he fought not to move while I went back to slowly torturing him with light grazes over the puckered skin. I pulled his ass cheeks apart, fully exposing his hole, and Derek whined at the sudden loss of contact. His protest stopped, and he inhaled sharply when my tongue made contact with the underside of his balls. I slowly licked a stripe from his balls, over his hole and up his crease, delighting in the babbling and whimpering falling from Derek's mouth.

I repeated the movement two more times with the same result. Derek's head hung low between his shoulders, rocking side to side, as he begged me to fuck him. The fourth time I licked him, I stopped at his hole, pushing my tongue in, allowing it to begin opening him up. Derek inhaled sharply as my tongue entered him and his fists beat at the floor.

By that point, I was fully hard, and precum was beading at the tip of my dick. I allowed myself a few extra minutes of tormenting him before sitting back on my heels. With my free hand, I gripped the base of my cock roughly.

"Please, please, please, Colt," Derek was begging between gritted teeth. A string of precum had formed at his slit and was dripping down, almost touching the towel. I knew he'd said he needed minimal prep, but a thorough tongue fucking did not good prep make. He was wet enough from my mouth that I didn't need to add lube as I slipped the first finger in. His body accepted my finger easily, practically swallowing it.

With my free hand, I grabbed the bottle of lube, fumbling to get it opened with one hand. The snick of the lid was loud in the room, but Derek didn't seem to notice as he continued to beg for *more* and *harder*. I removed all but the tip of my index finger and poured the lube down his crack so it coated my fingers before I drove into him with two.

"Fuuuuck," Derek groaned. "Fuck me, please, Colt. I need my ass filled, now."

I made sure to nail that sensitive bundle of nerves with my middle finger as I stretched him. Derek screamed his pleasure and begged for my cock, and I couldn't deny him any longer.

When I pulled out, he wiggled his hips and pushed back looking for more. I had a condom opened and my dick sheathed faster than I thought possible and grabbed the lube again to slick myself up more.

I carefully lined my tip up with his hole and slipped the head in. Derek was not in the mood to go slow and rocked back, pushing my cock into him until his ass hit my balls.

"Shit!" I hissed, as his body tightened around me. "Not going to last long, baby. You've got me ready to explode."

Derek began to rock himself back and forth. "Good, pound me. I'm so fucking ready. I need this, it's been too long." Pleasure radiated from his body and his arms began to shake. He dropped back down onto his elbows and allowed his head to hang low. Beads of sweat had gathered between his shoulder blades and at the base of his neck.

Little moans and rambles of *more* and *harder* and *please* kept escaping his mouth.

I pulled out almost all the way and slammed back into him. "YES!" he screamed when my balls hit his perineum again. I hoped there wasn't anyone in the connecting rooms.

"Fuck," I groaned, pistoning my hips in and out of him as fast as I could. An orgasm was already building in the base of my spine and I had just cum. With Derek's begging and his channel contracting greedily around me there was no way I was going to last more than a few minutes.

When I felt like I was getting close to the point of no return, I reached around his waist to grab his cock but he shook his head and batted my hand away. "No, please. Better this way." I didn't know if he was going to be able to get release without a hand, but I was too far gone to argue.

I pushed in one, two, three more times making sure to angle my thrusts to hit his gland just right before Derek let out a scream and his channel tightened around my aching cock. I felt his cock jump and hit my hand right before warm cum shot across it.

Holy fuck, the man just came untouched.

"Fuck. Yessss! Cum," he moaned as he pushed his ass into me a few more times.

The clenching of his ass around me sent me over the edge, and I let out a growl that would have woken up any neighboring rooms if Derek's screams hadn't already done so. I filled the condom, slowing my hips and allowing myself to ride out the pleasure as long as possible with short, shallow bucks of my hips.

"Damn, Sheriff, that was amazing," Derek told me with a yawn. "I've needed that."

I gripped the condom and gently pulled out, playfully smacking his ass. "I'll be right back." As I disposed of the condom in the bathroom, I tried to ignore the melancholy settling over me as I realized my time with Derek was coming to an end.

When I returned to Derek, he was sprawled out on the floor, lying on top of the cum splattered towel, almost asleep. "Hey, baby, why don't I tuck you in?" I asked quietly.

Derek nodded and pushed himself up, his taut muscles rippling with every movement and his thick flaccid cock swinging with each step. The man was incredibly sexy and he didn't seem to even know it.

I cleaned him up with a warm wet washcloth I had brought from the bathroom before he fell into bed. Pulling the blankets around him, I leaned over and brushed some hair from his face. "I'll let myself out," I whispered. "Sleep well, sweet boy."

"Wait," he mumbled, half asleep. "Give me your phone."

I was confused, but unlocked my phone and handed it over to him. I watched as he added his name and number to my contact list and sent a text. "Maybe next time I'm in town, we can catch up?" he questioned after a long yawn. "Maybe dinner?" he mumbled, as he drifted off to sleep.

It was a nice thought, though I knew our paths would likely never cross again. This night; however, was going to leave me with plenty of fantasies to keep me and my hand going for a while.

I got dressed and let myself out of the hotel room.

CHAPTER 5

DEREK

I WOKE UP TO SUN STREAMING IN THROUGH THE windows of my hotel room and a dull, but delicious, ache in my ass. As I rolled over, I remembered the night before. *Sheriff Colt Westfield.* My stomach did a little flip-flop thing at the thought of him. I really hoped I hadn't made a fool of myself the night before. It had been so long since I had been with a man that my logical brain had basically shut off the first time he called me a *good boy* at the bar.

He either had the best poker face ever or he really hadn't had a clue who I was. I was hoping for the latter because if it was the former he could potentially cause a PR nightmare for me. *I should warn Madeline,* I thought as I stumbled into the shower.

By the time I got out of the bathroom and got dressed, Madeline, my personal assistant, was sitting in my living room looking at the crumpled towels and my clothes on the floor as though they might bite her. "I'd ask how your night was, but I think I already figured it out," she said with a playful glint in her eye.

"What time is it?" I questioned, looking around for a clock, or my phone.

Madeline was already dressed for the day in a red blouse, purple pencil skirt, and red kitten heels. The toe of her right shoe was tapping impatiently on the floor and I looked at her in confusion.

"Why are you staring at me like that?" I asked. I needed coffee. "Did you bring coffee?" I inquired, looking around the room.

It was too early and I was too under-caffeinated to decipher her expression.

Madeline huffed and stood up, heading toward the small kitchen where she had placed a cup of coffee for me on the counter. She handed it over and tapped her foot, waiting me out.

"What?" I asked after I took the first sip of my coffee.

Her eyes widened in shock. "You *finally* get some and you don't even feel the need to tell me about it?" she scolded me.

I choked on my second sip from the cup. "Maddie!" I sputtered when I could breathe again.

"Don't you *Maddie* me, Derek Scott! I want to know the details." She leaned against the counter, crossing her shapely legs at the ankle and her arms over her ample chest.

I couldn't help but bark out a laugh. She had quickly become the sister I'd never had, and I had a tendency to forget she was my employee, not just a close friend.

She told me horror stories of some of her past clients—midnight runs to the grocery store for a pack of gum, three a.m. phone calls because they were drunk and couldn't remember what city they were in, much less where they should be. There had even been one client who had a very public breakdown and she had been on call around the clock for a week. I had made it a point to make her life as easy as possible when she signed on to my team. I had only called her once in the middle of the night because I had gotten food poisoning and needed to be taken to the hospital. I credited my respect for her as a person and not just as an employee, for our close friendship.

Sometimes, like at that moment, I questioned my decision because she felt she had the right to know all the finer details of my personal life.

Alright, I was being ridiculous, I knew I was going to tell her about Colt anyway.

I took another sip of my coffee and pulled myself up onto a stool in front of the little breakfast bar. "His name was Colt. Holy shit, the man was gorgeous. I met him at the bar last night when we all went out."

"And you brought him to the hotel?" she asked, raising a perfectly sculpted eyebrow in surprise.

I shrugged. "I kinda thought it would have been a bigger deal if I went back to his place, honestly. I don't think he had a clue who I was."

Madeline pursed her lips at me in disbelief. "You're telling me you really don't think this guy had a clue he fucked the brains out of the musician with the number one country single this week?"

"Hey! How do you know he fucked me and not the other way around? Wait, number one?" This was news to me. I knew we'd been climbing the charts with our latest single, but we'd been at number three the last two weeks. I thought we'd top out there. I still got excited when I thought about having a number one song on the radio.

She scoffed. "Um, because you're walking a little funny and you winced when you jumped up on the stool. You'd better hope you're feeling better before tonight's show."

It was my turn to laugh. "Okay, okay, you got me. I'll be fine by tonight. Maybe I'll take a long soak in the tub this afternoon before we have to go to the arena. In all seriousness, I'm telling you the truth, I don't think he had a clue who I was, but just in case, keep your eye on social media for any rumors that may spring up."

Madeline nodded. "I'll take your word for it. And thank you for being honest with me, it makes my job much easier when people tell me the truth!" She winked and took a sip of her coffee.

Madeline's praise didn't do anything for me and that got me thinking. I needed to do some more research on Daddy Doms. "Okay, get out of here, I need to eat some breakfast before things get crazy.

"Breakfast is in the oven. Don't burn yourself on the plate. I'll be back around three. Get some more rest, you look tired."

Maybe because I had just been ass up with Sheriff Westfield buried balls deep inside of me six hours ago.

I groaned. "See you this afternoon," I called at

Madeleine's retreating back before I turned and took my breakfast out of the oven.

I needed to find my phone before I did anything else. It was probably in my jeans and if I remembered correctly, Colt had taken them off me in front of the couch. I headed to the living room and found my pants and my cellphone in the back pocket of them. With my phone in my hand, I finally settled down to eat my breakfast.

There were five texts, a few emails, and one missed phone call. I quickly got through the emails, there was nothing important in those. There were texts from both of my brothers, my mom, Madeline, and a number I didn't recognize.

I figured it was safe to assume Madeline's text was no longer relevant since she had already been here. I would call my mom back in a minute, since she had called after texting me. My brothers could wait. I opened the text from the unknown number and read the two words on the screen: *Colt's number.* My heart dropped to my feet and I wasn't hungry anymore.

Shit, I must have been really out of it. Why did I give him my personal number? Madeline is going to kill me!

I paced as I tried to get my breathing under control.

What was I supposed to do with his number now that I knew I had it? Would he make the first move? What if he didn't call? Why did I care so much about a random hook-up?

Resigned, I flopped down on the couch and called my mom back. She had been my biggest supporter all my life. I was convinced Marla Scott was completely unflappable.

She had raised three boys, four if you counted my younger brother's best friend who was currently living at our house because his parents were shit, and had put up with my father for twenty-seven years. I was convinced if she were going to be ruffled by anything, it would have happened when I came out to her shortly before the tour started.

There had been so much going on in my life. My small-town, Oklahoma-boy identity had been about to be thrown out the window. I knew once the tour started, my life would never be the same. Unfortunately, country music fans aren't known for their acceptance of the LGBTQ community, and I was a gay man starting a country music career.

A few nights before I left on tour, my mom, little brother, Ty, and I sat in the kitchen talking. Over the course of a few hours, my mom had poured us a few shots of scotch and I had managed to get a nice buzz going. When she asked me how I was feeling about the tour, I had meant to say, "I'm nervous," but what came out was, "I'm gay."

Ty pumped his fist. "I knew it!" he said triumphantly.

My mom nodded once, drained her cup, and said the last thing I would have ever expected her to say. "I slept with your Uncle Joe once, shortly before I started dating your dad."

"Eww!" Ty wrinkled up his nose. "I don't want to think about you and Dad doing the deed, but you did it with his brother too." He shuddered. "Gross!"

"It was one time." She shrugged. "I was sixteen, he was eighteen. It was after a school bonfire."

"Lalalalala," Ty yelped, sticking his fingers in his ears.

The two asked me how long I had known and why I hadn't said anything before, but after that, the confessions were over and it was like nothing had changed.

When my dad found out, he lectured me on the "perils of homosexuality" and tried to tell me he could set up a meeting with the church pastor for guidance. He also asked me to cancel the tour to seek therapy. I refused his help and he hadn't spoken to me since. We hadn't been all that close before I left home and I didn't feel like I was missing much, but it still stung sometimes.

"Derek!" My mom's voice rang out through the phone as she picked up after the first ring. "What are you up to?"

I smiled, she was always so excited to hear from me. I had just spoken to her three days ago, but you'd think it had been three months. "Nothing much. Long night last night, still pretty tired. Hopefully, I can sleep a bit after lunch before I have to get to the arena." Long nights were nothing new for me, so, thankfully, she didn't question it or press for more. I didn't really want to tell her I picked a guy up in a bar and brought him back to my hotel.

We talked for another ten minutes. She hit on everything she deemed important—How was I feeling? Was the hotel nice? Would I get a break soon? I gave her my usual responses—Great, but tired. Very nice, as always. And a scoff with a promise I'd make it back before I died. She teasingly asked if I'd met anyone, like she did every conversation, and I brushed off her question just like I always did, promising she would be the first to know if someone caught my eye. When she was satisfied I was doing well, she passed the phone to Ty, and then my older brother, Jasper. We each talked for a few minutes before I was able to make my excuses.

After disconnecting with my family, I relaxed back into the couch and closed my eyes, remembering how sexy Colt had been when he went all, well, Daddy Dom on me the night before. I was ready to go to a place I hadn't let myself explore since I discovered the kink. I got up and grabbed my laptop bag. I was finally ready to understand more about Daddy/boy relationships and why I was drawn to them.

I'd been curious about the relationship dynamics for years. I'd stumbled across a Reddit post about a Daddy Dom and his boy my freshman year of college. From my first glimpse of the lifestyle, I'd been drawn to the love and attentiveness of it. The pictures of both the Daddy and his boy in leather were unlike anything I'd seen before. The boy was curled up on his Daddy's lap with his head resting on his shoulder while his Daddy was looking down at him with a tender smile on his face.

Since then, I'd wanted someone who would look at me like that; like I was the most precious thing in their life. The guys I'd dated in the past always seemed to think I wanted to top, or that I should have been, at the very least, more dominant. When I tried to curl up with them in the evening or lay my head in their laps, they got weird about it. I learned quickly not to tell a guy I didn't want to—or worse yet, *couldn't*—make a decision.

The same day I'd come across the Reddit thread, I'd discovered age play relationships. I knew very little about that type of relationship or lifestyle, but that was because when I'd come across it I was so intrigued, I refused to explore it further. It had scared me how easily I could put myself in the boy's place. Even the diapers and other childish items I'd stumbled across weren't as off-putting as they should have been. I'd been so afraid of why I was drawn to it that I'd never let myself go back down that path. I'd convinced myself there was no way I'd ever find that type of relationship in Oklahoma. Once we started touring there'd been no way I could seek out that sort of lifestyle. It was best left unexplored.

Until that morning.

Colt had been a take charge kind of man. He exuded dominance in everything from the way he held himself to how he spoke. He'd called me a good boy enough times that I strongly suspected he was a Daddy. Now that I accepted Daddies may not be some mythical creature of the fetish world, I wanted to know more about age play and regression. I wanted to know if I could see myself in that position.

Opening a new browser tab I typed the two words I'd never let myself type before: age play.

I settled back on the couch and I had just found a blog written by a boy about his relationship with his Daddy when my phone pinged beside me.

Ty: *Spill, who'd you meet?*

Me: *What?*

Ty: *That nervous cough thing you did may have satis-fied Mom, but I know you better!*

Me: *You weren't even on the phone!*

Ty: I was close enough to hear you. You're deflecting.

Me: Even if I did meet someone, it isn't like it was anything more than a one time thing.

Ty: But you want it to be.

Me: Doesn't matter. He lives near Nashville.

Ty: So there IS someone!

Fuck, I'd said too much.

Me: Goodbye Ty. Love you.

And there went my concentration. I decided to take a nap then hit the gym before going to the arena. Since being on tour, the only way I ever got time to myself was if I put earbuds in and either ran or lifted weights. I liked having time to myself and as a result my ass was now firmer and my biceps and chest had packed on so much muscle I had to buy dress shirts a size up. My waist had slimmed down to the point I was paying someone to alter my jeans. I had tried to go down a size, but my butt and thighs hadn't fit in them. Even I could admit I was looking pretty damn good since I started going to the gym more often.

CHAPTER 6

COLT

ELISE: MOM WON'T LET ME GO TO THE HOMETOWN *concert tonight unless you go :-/*

Me: *What is Hometown?*

Elise: *Colton!*

I could actually hear my little sister dragging out my name in a groan.

Me: *Ellie, I don't know what or who Hometown is. Why won't Mom let you go without me?*

Elise: *The hottest band in country music! And the lead singer is gorgeous! That should be enough to get you to go with me.*

Me: *Who is going?*

Why was I even entertaining this? I was going to feel every day of thirty-six if I went to a concert with my sixteen-year-old sister and her friends tonight. I was already tired from being out until after two with Derek last night.

Derek...

Elise: *Jaina. Her older sister was going to take us, but she's sick. Mom won't let me go without an adult and she and dad don't want to go to Nashville tonight.*

Me: *You owe me, Elise.*

Elise: *THANK YOU THANK YOU THANK YOU THANK YOU!!!!!!!!!!! We need to leave at 5!*

I sighed. It was a good thing I was already off today. I was going to need to nap if I was taking two sixteen-year-old girls to a concert tonight. Man, was I getting old.

ELISE AND JAINA were in my living room at 4:30 bouncing up and down and begging me to hurry up.

"Mom, what did I do to deserve this?" I groaned as I pulled a new shirt over my head.

She sighed into the phone. "Your dad and I already have *plans* tonight."

The way she emphasized the word plans sent a chill down my spine, and not in a good way. "Oh god, Mom! TMI!" I yelped. "Eww, there are some things a kid just doesn't need to know about their parents, no matter how old they are!"

Mom laughed maniacally.

"You owe me, big time—for this concert *and* that over-share," I told her before I disconnected the call and grabbed my phone from my dresser. I debated about texting Derek to see what he was doing that night. Maybe I could talk him in to meeting up after the show. I quickly dismissed the thought, I needed to act like an adult chaperone to two teenage girls, I couldn't be thinking about a potential hook-up.

"Colton James Westfield, get your ass moving!" Elise yelled from my living room.

"Watch the language, young lady," I teased her as I stepped out of my room to find my boots. "Need I remind you that you two are a full *half an hour* early?"

After I put my boots on and grabbed my keys, we headed for the truck.

"Shotgun!" Elise yelled as my SUV came into view.

"You know it would be polite for you to sit in the back with your friend," I snarked at her.

"But then I wouldn't be able to control the radio. Can I connect my phone to your BlueTooth?" Elise asked as I started the truck. "We want to listen to Hometown's album."

I refrained from telling them that, at their age, I was listening to CDs. *Shit, when did I get so old?* I simply nodded to her and let her do her thing.

Halfway to Nashville, I was ready to admit the lead singer of the band had a good voice and was hopeful the concert wouldn't be a total dumpster fire. She honestly could have picked a much worse band to drag me to see.

I didn't bother to ask how Elise had managed to get tickets so close to the stage, but we were only about ten rows back. I was just thankful we had seats. The longer the night went on, the more exhausted I became. It was time to admit I was too old to stay out so late two nights in a row.

The opening acts weren't bad, but the energy in the

arena shifted as Hometown got ready to go on. Elise and Jaina both jumped up and screamed when Hometown took the stage. I didn't have much interest in the band, though there was something familiar about the lead singer's voice I couldn't quite place.

"Good evening, Nashville!" he said after the opening number, and the arena erupted in ear splitting cheers. "It's so great to be back here for a second night," he said once the noise died down to a loud rumble.

"He is so hot!" I heard Elise yell to her friend and I couldn't help but roll my eyes at them.

The high pitched squeal a teenage girl can omit for their crush should have it's own decibel rating. *Baby crying. Car horn. Airplane taking off. Teenaged-girl squeal.* I laughed at myself.

"Colt, stand up! You are not going to act like Dad at a concert. I am sure even you can appreciate how gorgeous Derek Edwards is!" Elise yelled during the second song.

I stood as her words hit me hard. *Derek* Edwards. There was no way, but there were too many coincidences —*show business, busy schedules, around here often.* I glanced up to see the back side of the blonde-haired lead singer as he walked toward a petite singer with purple hair. The *same* purple hair I had seen on the girl who walked into the bar with Derek the night before...

Being in law enforcement for so long, I picked up on subtle details of everyday situations others missed. Of course, the bright purple hair wasn't exactly subtle, but I distinctly remembered the short, spiky style.

The singer reached her, they had a short back and

forth exchange through body language, and I could hear his chuckle over the sound system as he continued to sing. I already knew what I was going to see when he turned back around, but my breath caught when he did. The same blonde mop of curls and stunning blue eyes from last night came into view.

"Fuck," I exhaled not realizing I had been holding my breath while I gaped at the man on the stage in disbelief.

"Colt," Elise poked at my shoulder as I stared slack-jawed at the stage. "Colt, what's wrong? It looks like you've seen a ghost." She was standing on her tiptoes and pulling my shoulder down so she could yell into my ear. "Are you okay?"

"I...yeah, I'm fine." I blinked, still looking at Derek. The sexy, beautiful man who had my cock down his throat eighteen hours earlier.

"Colt, you look like you're about to be sick." I could see Elise really was worried about me.

"I'm fine, Ellie. I was just surprised for a minute, I thought he was someone I knew. I'm obviously mistaken."

My sister laughed at me. "Yeah, right. He hasn't been arrested and he's only been in Tennessee for two days. You don't get out enough to bump into someone famous," she teased.

"Yeah," I tried to laugh. "You're right."

I pulled my phone out of my pocket and scrolled through my contacts. "Derek" was there, second name in the D section. Right under the contact labeled *Dad*. I switched to the camera app and waited until Derek turned toward us, then I snapped a clear picture of his face.

I tapped out a quick text and attached the picture.

_Me_: *Well, I wasn't expecting this.*

CHAPTER 7

DEREK

I bounced down the steps at 9:58 p.m. dripping sweat and anxious to find a shower. After high fiving the band and crew members, I power-walked down the hall to my dressing room and slipped inside. I had my shirt and jeans peeled off my body and the water in the shower running when a notification on my phone caught my eye.

Damn it, I was going to have to check it or else it would drive me nuts until I got out of the shower. That stupid notification would ruin my shower if I didn't know what was waiting for me. It could have been anything from a funny meme from Ty or Jasper to a junk email. No matter what, I had to know.

I swiped up and entered my password, then spent the next two minutes staring at a picture of me on stage. The picture appeared right below the text I had sent myself that morning and right above the words, *Well, I wasn't expecting this.*

I was sure he had no clue who I was the night before,

53

but then he showed up at my concert, apparently pretty close to the stage. *What the hell?* Despite my brain telling me this wasn't a good idea, my dick was already screaming for round two.

I hit reply before I could overthink my response.

Me: *Where are you?*

I was surprised when my phone pinged with a response almost immediately.

Colt: *In hell, thanks.*

Me: *What?*

Colt: *I'm walking to my truck with my sister and her best friend.*

Colt: *Listening to them squawk about how* dreamy *Derek Edwards is.*

It hit me I knew next to nothing about Colt Westfield. I knew he was a local sheriff. I knew he looked amazing in his uniform. He had a dick that could send me to places I'd never been before. And, now I knew he had a little sister. *Huh, those are weird things to know about a person.* I hesitated a beat before sending the next text.

Me: *Come back?*

Colt: *What?*

Me: *I'll get you guys backstage. Come to the back of the arena. I'll tell security to let you in. Just show them your ID.*

Colt: *I'd love to come back, but I'm not about to subject any of us to the hell that would accompany my starstruck sister and her best friend. I'll call my brother, see if he can meet me halfway to get the girls? Then I'll swing back your way. Hopefully only an hour or so...*

Me: *Sounds good. Text me when you're close, I'll let you know where I'm at.*

Honestly, I liked this plan more anyway. I wanted to talk with Colt more than flirt that night, but to talk openly was going to require privacy.

CHAPTER 8

COLT

WHAT THE FUCK AM I DOING?

I told my sister and brother something had come up and I needed to get back to Nashville. Thankfully, due to my work, no one questioned me, but it still made me feel bad for lying to them. I just didn't quite know how to tell them the lead singer of Hometown invited me to his dressing room. That would lead to far too many questions and I didn't have decent answers for any of them.

When I finally met up with Mitch to transfer Elise and Jaina over to him, I was eighteen minutes from the arena. Of course, it had taken me thirty to get that far because of traffic, but going back toward Nashville I didn't expect the traffic to be that bad.

Before I got back on the road, I texted Derek with an ETA. He told me to go back to the hotel we were at the night before, and he would meet me at the private entrance when I got there.

I had no idea what to expect from Derek that night.

Was last night a one time thing?

Did he want more?

Every thought I had caused more questions to spring up in my mind.

Pulling into the parking lot, I snaked around to the back and parked under the same light I had the night before. As I got to the door, Derek opened it and smiled. He wasn't dressed up that night. Instead, he looked comfortable in a pair of well worn gray sweatpants and a navy blue hoodie with the words "Pleasant High School, Class of 2012" printed across the chest. If that was his sweatshirt, and I had no reason to believe it wasn't, that made me twelve years older than Derek.

"Hey, I'm glad you came back. Thank you," he said as soon as the door was closed behind me.

I needed to find my inner Dom because I was going to make a bumbling mess of this and embarrass myself if I didn't. "Thank you for inviting me back."

We entered the elevator and Derek drew in a breath, raking his hands through his hair causing it to stick out. "Uh, so hi, I'm Derek Scott." He laughed nervously.

"Derek Scott? My sister kept calling you Derek Edwards."

"Edward is my middle name. The record label thought Derek Edwards was more marketable when we were first starting out. So, the public knows me as Derek Edwards." He glanced up at me with uneasy eyes. "I didn't think you knew who I was last night."

I shook my head. "I didn't know who you were until the second song of the concert tonight. My sister got the tickets and she wanted to take her best friend. Their chaperon got sick at the last minute and my parents wouldn't let two sixteen-year-olds come up here on their own, so Elise begged me to come with them tonight. She's lucky I didn't have to work."

"Well, it gave me a chance to see you again too. I think I may be the lucky one." He was radiating nervousness and I found it endearing. He was adorable when he got flustered. The tips of his ears turned red, he dropped his chin to his chest, and sucked his bottom lip between his teeth.

I wanted to gather him in my arms and kiss his forehead. The admission was tender and sweet. I was quickly realizing Derek had a tendency to wear his heart on his sleeve, at least around me. I forced myself to keep my distance from him, but I couldn't keep the tenderness out of my voice when I responded. "That was very sweet of you to say. I'm glad you texted back."

"I'm sorry," he blurted out as the elevator came to a stop on the sixth floor.

His apology surprised me. "Why are you sorry?"

Derek didn't say anything as the doors slid open and we made our way to his room. He scanned his keycard and let us in. We weren't all over each other like we'd been the night before and there were questions hanging in the air between us. We were going to need to have a long conversation before we could even think about letting this visit turn sexy. But, watching Derek shuffle nervously from foot-to-foot, I wasn't going to deny my continued interest in him.

"I didn't tell you who I was last night. I feel guilty about that."

I took the lead and walked us over to the couch. Derek sat down beside me so his arm was just brushing mine. "Thank you, but there is no need to apologize for that, baby," I winced at my words. *Why did this man bring my Daddy Dom out so naturally?* Thankfully, Derek didn't seem to notice my slip. He seemed to be somewhere else completely, so I reached over and touched his leg. "You need to protect yourself. I understand your privacy is important to you."

Derek looked up at me, his bottom lip was swollen from where he had been chewing on it. "I-I don't remember giving you my number last night," he admitted. "But, I'm glad I did."

I felt myself smile and my voice was tender. "I'm glad about that, too."

If he chewed on his lip much more, I was afraid he was going to draw blood. I reached up and tugged gently at his lower lip to remove it from his teeth. "If you keep that up, I'm going to have to go find you a pacifier. You're going to chew through your lip."

Jesus Christ, Colt, control yourself!

Before I could correct myself, I saw Derek's body language change. He didn't seem so uncertain anymore. His blue eyes met mine and I detected a bit of a challenge in them. He gave me a sexy, confident smirk then waggled his eyebrows. "Oh, really?"

Was he teasing me?

I nodded, seeing how far he would want to play along.

"I can't let you hurt those gorgeous lips. It would be much harder to kiss them if they were cracked and raw."

Derek put his finger on his chin and pretended to think. "Can we try the kiss first? Then discuss ways to protect my delicate lips?"

He leaned in and brushed his lips against mine. I let him explore my lips for a few seconds before I took control, pushing him back slightly as I traced the seam of his lips with my tongue. Derek's dominant streak ended there as he parted his lips on a sigh and moaned into my mouth.

I let the kiss linger for a few more minutes. When I felt him move closer, his hand moving to my chest, I pulled back. "You got your kiss, now we need to have a discussion."

Derek sat back in surprise. He apparently hadn't expected an actual discussion. "Um, sure? What do you want to talk about?"

"First off, last night was incredible and I am not opposed to a repeat performance tonight."

Derek grinned. "Well we are in agreement there."

"I would, however, like to talk about some boundaries."

"Boundaries?" He looked intrigued, but a little skeptical.

How did I even begin bringing up my Daddy Dom side to someone who may or may not be familiar with the lifestyle. At a club, it was easy because everyone was kinky. At my regular fetish club, I wore a nametag and I always included that I was a Daddy Dom on it. In the real world, it wasn't so easy. I ran the risk of scaring him away completely. My logical brain kicked in and reminded me that my Daddy Dom was too much a part of me to ignore. I would never be happy in a relationship without letting him out to play. If Derek wasn't interested in what I had to offer, then this wasn't meant to be.

"Boundaries, yes, but I also want to understand your interests." I responded. "We never talked about what you were comfortable with last night. I hadn't really thought it was going to be a problem since it was supposed to be a one-time hook-up. Last night, you seemed to look to me quite often for...direction."

Derek blushed and his lip got sucked back under his top teeth. "No, none of that," I told him gently as I pulled the lip from his teeth again. "You also seemed to like to please me quite a bit."

Derek didn't even have to think about that one, he nodded eagerly.

"There is no easy way to ask this question, but I feel like we need to discuss it before we continue tonight. There is no right or wrong answer to this, but it will give *me* an idea of what *you* are looking to get out of this."

Derek seemed more hesitant than before, but he nodded again in understanding.

"Good boy," I said out of habit. It was already so automatic around him it was going to be difficult if he told me that he wasn't, at the very least, submissive. "Derek, are you a submissive?" I asked him. The question was blunt and to the point, but it left no room for him to give me a half answer.

Derek blinked up at me. "Sometimes? Not always... A

little... I guess?" he hedged before looking back to his lap. Okay, I was wrong, he *could* give me an indirect answer.

I chuckled. "Care to elaborate?"

Derek pulled his lip into his mouth for a second, but before I could correct him, he let it out and reached for the blanket on the back of the couch. He pulled it into his lap and rubbed the hem of it while he thought of how to answer. "I-I am sometimes submissive. It isn't an all the time thing for me. Some nights, I just like to be told what to do so I can let go of everything weighing on me. Last night was one of those nights. It had been months since I'd been with anyone, even longer since I'd been submissive in any way."

He stopped for a moment, then clarified his thoughts. "I may be submissive, but I don't like to be whipped, tied, or bound. That's just not my thing. And the thought of kneeling before someone weirds me out."

"Would you say that you enjoy feeling cared for?"

Derek's blue eyes widened and I wondered if he knew where I was leading this conversation. It took him a moment but he nodded. "Yeah. Is that weird?"

"It may be weird to some people, but it makes perfect sense to me. I learned a few years ago I'm a Dom, but it took me a while to figure out why having a sub kneel at my feet or beg to be whipped and paddled did nothing for me."

Derek was watching me intently. Nervous energy was radiating off him. The little movements in his face—the way his eyes crinkled slightly at the corners and the almost imperceptible way his brow turned downward—made me think the nervousness was more of an anxious anticipation. That hope people got when someone understood what they were talking about without the need to spell it out. I hoped what I was about to tell him made him feel confident.

"Why was that?" He seemed to be holding his breath for my answer.

"I'm a Daddy Dom. I like to care for my submissives, *my boys,* on a more emotional level. I find the most pleasure in knowing my boy can come to me whenever he needs me. Even if it's just for a hug or a cuddle. I don't mind disciplining a boy who's been naughty, but I'd rather he be over my knee for a spanking and I prefer to use my hand over a paddle or whip."

Derek sank back on the couch, tension and nerves seeping out of his body and appearing to leave him as wrung out and exhausted as his orgasm had the night before. "You get it," he whispered.

I nodded. "I do." Now that I knew for certain we were on the same page, I relaxed and wrapped my right arm around his shoulders, pulling him into my side.

Derek practically burrowed into me, bringing the blanket with him. After a few minutes he was so relaxed I wondered if he had fallen asleep. He finally looked up at me, "Thank you, I needed this. I hadn't really been able to explain what I wanted to anyone before, but you just understood. It's so...nice."

I bent down and kissed the top of his head. "Anytime." It struck me that I meant it, but it would be almost impossible with his tour schedule. "Do you know anything about the age play and regression that sometimes coexist with the Daddy/boy lifestyle?"

Derek's body tensed slightly in my arms, and his finger started working the hem of the blanket again. He seemed to have a number of subconscious soothing mechanisms making it easy for me to picture him on the floor playing with toys and looking to his Daddy for comfort and guidance.

I rubbed his shoulder as he processed my question, not willing to rush whatever was worrying him. He needed to work this one out in his own way.

Derek finally gave a little shrug and spoke into my chest, making me have to strain to hear his soft words. "I know they sometimes go hand-in-hand, but I don't know much about age play."

Honesty was always the best policy and since this would be the last chance Derek and I had to explore this I decided to jump in with both feet. "Would you be interested in being Daddy's boy tonight?"

Derek's head shot up in surprise. "What does that mean exactly? You mean, y-you want me to be, little? H-how little?" He went still.

CHAPTER 9

DEREK

WHEN COLT FIRST STARTED EXPLAINING TO ME THAT he liked a more gentle form of domination, I couldn't believe what I was hearing.

Had I really found my unicorn?

It didn't surprise me much when he told me he was a Daddy. It was evident in his every action—he'd unbuckled my seat belt, opened my door, and even tucked me in before he left for the night. The way he wrapped me in his arms felt so natural, I'd never wanted to move. All of those things made sense for a man who identified as a Daddy Dom.

Then he surprised me by bringing up age play.

Understanding I liked to submit was easy enough; after watching a handful of porn videos I had the submission thing figured out. My obsession with my ass and ass play from puberty on was a fairly good indication I preferred to bottom. Not that there was anything wrong with topping, because I did it from time to time and I enjoyed it when I did. There was just something about being six feet tall with submissive tendencies and a preference to bottom, that was hard for a lot of guys to wrap their heads around.

Since the start of the tour, my fantasies had shifted to me submitting more often than not. I tried not to read too much into it, usually. Having to always be camera ready and knowing I couldn't let my guard down had begun taking its toll on me. I wanted someone to take that responsibility away from me. I wanted to be able to just let go and just be in the moment.

For the first few months of the tour, the fantasy was a lot like what Colt and I had done the night before. As the tour continued, my fantasy had changed. I kept thinking about the age play site I'd found. It was getting easier and easier to put myself in the place of Daddy's little boy. It scared me a little how easily I could see myself in that role. I would be able to escape, Daddy would take control. I could enjoy "little" things that still made me happy, but I hid from everyone—watching cartoons, building with LEGO bricks, sleeping with my blanket—without worrying about being judged.

My mind was whirling and I caught my thumb rising to my mouth. I pulled it down before it made it to my lips. It had been almost eight years since I'd given up that habit. Everyone had been so relieved when I finally stopped. *Okay, everyone but me.* I had always found comfort in sucking my thumb, but I got tired of my dad barking at me and my older brother teasing me, so I forced myself to stop around the house. I still let my thumb slip into my mouth when I was in bed until I was almost sixteen. I was twenty-four and I was not about to start again. I glared down at my thumb for a moment, forgetting what I had originally been contemplating.

Colt must have noticed something in my body language because his finger started tracing soothing patterns on my arm and down the portion of my back he could reach.

Did I want to be his little boy for the night?

The way my dick was coming to life, it was definitely on board. It wasn't so much the thought of being little that was turning me on, but the thought of escaping into a reality where I could just let go. Where I wouldn't have to be Derek Edwards, country superstar and I could just...be. My heart was ready to beat out of my chest with the anticipation of letting my mind be that free for once. The doubt demons that were always at the forefront of my thoughts had even gone quiet. There was something about Colt I trusted implicitly, even after so short a time, that was the only reason why I could even be entertaining this.

I nodded without even realizing it.

"Is that a yes?" Colt's silent laugh vibrated in his chest.

"Um, how little?" I asked, venturing to look up at his face.

Colt looked around the room and thought for a minute. "Well, we don't have a lot of the staples that would be common for age play at our disposal tonight. But, maybe we can watch some cartoons and cuddle?"

He looked around the room again. "Do you, by chance, have any paper and crayons or pencils, or even pens?"

"I have a sketch pad and some colored pencils," I offered.

"We could turn the TV on and you could draw a picture," he offered.

My brain had apparently jumped at the idea of shutting off, because the next thing out of my mouth surprised even me. "And a bath?"

Colt gave me a soft smile that made my stomach do funny things. "I would love to give you a bath if you want one."

I nodded. The few times that I had really thought about what I would want from a Daddy, I always envisioned my Daddy lovingly washing my hair and body while I was in the bathtub. I couldn't think of a way to show more submission and trust than to let someone bathe me.

"Is there anything else you want to talk about before we start?" Colt questioned.

I shook my head. There was plenty I wanted to know, but it was all practical experience from here on out.

"When we get up from the couch, I'm no longer Colt. You will call me Daddy. Do you understand?"

I knew enough to know I needed to answer the question clearly. "You will be Daddy once we start playing."

A smile tugged at Colt's lips. It was the first time I had noticed he had a dimple in each cheek. "Good boy. I don't plan on pushing you very far tonight, but if things get uncomfortable, we'll use traffic light signals. Are you familiar with them?"

I nodded. "Green for good, yellow means slow down so we can talk about what's happening, and red for stop."

"Yes. If you say red, everything stops immediately. No judgment, no questions."

"Got it."

Colt's voice dropped lower with the next words and I knew it was game on. "Time to color and watch cartoons."

CHAPTER 10

COLT

Derek stood and shifted awkwardly, clearly unsure of what to do. I stood and took his hand. "Show me where your coloring stuff is." I needed to come up with a nickname for him, but I was failing at the moment. He didn't strike me as a *boy, baby,* or *little one.* I didn't want to call him Derek either. I was going to avoid using a nickname until something felt right, I just hoped it came to me soon.

Derek looked up at me and nodded. "On my bed. I was sketching earlier."

Leading him by the hand, I headed toward the bedroom. It was definitely more lived in that evening than the night before. A small pile of clothes had accumulated on the chair in the corner, his laptop was perched on the dresser, a guitar case rested against the wall by the bed, and half the bed was unmade. Sitting on the, mainly undisturbed, side of the bed was a sketchbook and a set of colored pencils.

Derek's hand tightened around mine. "Let Daddy gather your stuff and we'll go back to the living room so you can color a picture."

My sweet boy's head bobbed up and down as he chewed his bottom lip. If he chewed his lip like this normally, I was surprised it wasn't constantly chapped. If his little side was naturally nervous, he was going to need a pacifier.

Derek didn't seem to be ready to let my hand go, so I gathered his colored pencils and sketchbook with my free hand. Once I had them, I turned to see Derek's embarrassed face staring back at me.

I had to remind myself this was all new to Derek. The boy standing next to me, with a vise-like grip on my hand, had never shared this side of himself with another person. He was, likely, equal parts excited and terrified about the evening. As his Daddy, it was my job to calm his nerves and allow him to explore his role as far as he was comfortable.

On instinct, I placed a gentle kiss on his forehead. "Have you thought about what you want to draw?" I asked him as we started back toward the living room.

His rapid head shake showed how nervous he was.

"Do you like animals?" I asked him, trying to keep my tone light.

Derek shrugged. "I guess."

That wasn't a ringing endorsement, so I went for the next thought. "What about cars?"

He hedged and nodded. "Yeah." It was still hesitant,

but not as non-committal as the first suggestion. "I like trains a lot," he said as we reached the living room.

"Oh you do?" I asked, trying to sound surprised but not like I was forcing it.

Derek nodded. "Yeah. People always get mad about getting stuck by a train, but I kinda like it. The sound is soothing. It's rhythmic and predictable."

Just talking about the trains seemed to relax Derek and blood was beginning to flow to my hand again as he loosened his grip. I set the book and the pencils down on the coffee table and walked us closer to the couch. There was a throw pillow resting in the corner and I tossed it onto the floor so he would be more comfortable.

"Sit down so Daddy can turn on cartoons." I was trying to make him feel like what we were doing was completely normal.

Derek nodded and reluctantly let go of my hand to ease himself down onto the pillow. Once he had settled into his spot, I pushed the supplies closer to him. "Will you draw a train picture?"

The tip of Derek's tongue poked out from between his lips as he nodded. He reached for his pencils and his brows turned downward as he began to think about his picture. Before he could get too engrossed in his drawing, I grabbed the remote.

"Cartoons?"

"Please," he nodded as he glanced up to the TV.

"Please what, buddy?" *Huh, that name was fitting and flowed naturally.*

Derek's blue eyes brightened and a small smile spread

on his lips. *And he liked it, even better.* It was easy to see Derek as my buddy, and if that thought didn't come out of nowhere.

"Please... Daddy," he managed after more than a brief pause.

I smiled. "Good boy." Derek seemed to sit up taller at the compliment. *When was the last time someone praised him outside of his job?* I knew it was important to let him color and explore his interests, but I wanted to wrap my arms around him and hold him for the rest of the night. I'd have showered him with praise and told him how perfect he was if I thought that was what he really needed right then. Instead, I made a mental note to praise him as often as was possible.

I settled myself onto the couch and turned on the TV. I'd flipped through numerous channels and stopped briefly on each cartoon to see if it was something Derek wanted to watch. He shook his head at the cartoons meant for adults, as well as the classics. I finally got to the channels geared toward kids and noticed he began to watch the channels intently. I slowed down even more, giving him plenty of time to see what was on the channel before he'd inevitably shake his head.

He'd already dismissed shows about mischievous puppies, little fish at school, and a different puppy show before I landed on a show about pajama clad superheroes.

"This one, Daddy!" he announced, pointing excitedly at the TV. I'd never seen it, then again, I didn't care for cartoons, but Derek was certain this was the one wanted. The ease with which he had called me "Daddy" when he saw the show had already made me like it, at least a little.

Once we'd found a show he liked, Derek seemed to shut everything else out. His attention stayed between the show and his picture. Every few minutes, he would look toward me, seeming to check I was still there, before he would focus back on his work.

He let two full episodes of the show play before he began to stretch. In that time, I'd watched him closely. His shoulders had relaxed, he wasn't chewing his lip, and each time he caught my eye, he'd grin before returning to his work.

Each little giggle at the cartoon, or happy smile shot my way, endeared him to me a little more. I could see myself spending evenings with him as he colored in my living room or played with toys on the floor. I'd gladly trade the quiet of my house for the sound of his giggles filling the room.

After an hour, he was clearly uncomfortable. With his height, I was surprised he had made it that long without moving around. He gave me a hesitant glance then averted his eyes while he chewed his lip.

Before I could ask him what was wrong, he managed to find the courage to blurt out, "Can I please have a bath, Daddy?"

Even though he had mentioned having a bath earlier, I was surprised at his request. It had been hard for him to find the courage to draw a picture an hour earlier. It was possible he'd sunk into a little space that easily, but I suspected he was trying to gain as many experiences as possible while he had the chance.

The fact that he'd opened up to me about his desires in the first place was surprising enough, and, I hoped I let him know he was safe with me. There weren't going to be many, if any, chances for him to be little again, especially while he was on tour. We'd happened upon each other in a bar and it was like fate had brought us together. Derek had never gotten to experience regression and I was happy to let him explore any aspect of it he wanted. It couldn't be easy knowing you desired something outside of the box. Being in the spotlight, one wrong move, one wrong word, and the life he knew could crumble away.

I could provide him a safe space to explore his little side, and I was happy to give him the opportunity with no judgment from me.

And if that didn't leave me with a weird ache in my stomach.

It was rapidly becoming harder for me to accept this as a short-term arrangement.

Choosing to ignore my feelings, I stood up. "Let's go get you in the bathtub, buddy. I love your picture. You did a very nice job on it."

Derek smiled and a light pink stained his cheeks. "Thank you."

I waited for him to get to his feet before I took his hand. Despite his nerves, he was radiating joy and by the time we got to the bathroom, he was nearly bouncing with excitement. He was more ready for this than I had expected.

I took a minute and tried to put myself in Derek's shoes, but couldn't. Even imagining being in the spotlight and having to always be on my best behavior was daunting. Kingfield was a small enough area everyone seemed to know everyone else *and* their business. Even knowing I couldn't go to the grocery store without someone stopping me could be overwhelming at times. Derek was the lead singer of a wildly successful country band and had fans and photographers following his every move. It wasn't surprising to me he was curious about what being little would be like and it was far less surprising he leaned toward the submissive end of the spectrum.

I had met a number of subs in my lifetime who were successful—CEOs, CFOs, even politicians. They had all been drawn to submission because it gave them a chance to *not* be in control. Exploring a little lifestyle was taking the ability to let go to a different level. The boy standing in front of me was begging to be cared for.

CHAPTER 11

DEREK

THE HOTEL BATHROOM PUT MOST HOME BATHROOMS to shame. I was vaguely aware the large soaking tub was the perfect size for me, yet it was hard to care that much. My head felt fuzzy and I really just wanted to be in the tub. I couldn't figure out why Colt was studying the little bottles of shampoo, conditioner, and other toiletries that had been placed on the counter. After what seemed like hours, but was probably only seconds, he hissed out a satisfied "Yes!" and turned around to start the water.

Since the tub was now filling, I took that as my cue to undress. I'd only managed to get the drawstring untied before Colt turned around and saw what I was doing. "Wait buddy, that's Daddy's job," he explained gently. I thought I should have been embarrassed by him stepping forward and pushing my hands away, but all I could think about was how easy it was to think of him as my Daddy and how much I liked being his buddy.

I knew there was a bulge in the front of my sweatpants

that wasn't hiding how much I liked what was happening. Even though my cock was hard, I didn't feel the need, or desire, for release. It felt like I was outside my body, watching as Daddy undressed me. He did a great job of ignoring my erection. That warm, slightly fuzzy feeling I had while I was coloring was tightening its grip on me, making it hard to focus on my arousal.

I was completely naked and impatiently rocking back and forth on the balls of my feet before I realized Daddy had been happy because he'd found bubble bath on the counter. There were large mountains of bubbles filling the tub almost to the top edge. Daddy hummed his approval and turned the water off.

He offered me a hand. "All right, buddy, in you get."

I took his hand as I stepped into the tub and sank down into the water. How Daddy managed to ignore the erection that was pointing toward my belly button like an arrow, was beyond me. I didn't care much either—there were mounds of bubbles waiting to be played with.

"You play with the bubbles for a few minutes while I find a washcloth and get some soap," Daddy explained as he turned around. He didn't have to tell me twice, I was already scooping the bubbles up with my hands and piling them as high as I could.

"Hey, look at this. Here's something you can play with," Daddy announced triumphantly as he dropped to his knees in front of the tub. I watched as he dunked the cup into the bubbles and pulled out a large scoop dumping them on top of another mound. They stayed on the top and I felt myself grin widely. Part of me realized I hadn't grinned so much in years, but most of me just wanted to play in the tub.

"I'll leave this in your capable hands." He handed over the cup and booped me on the nose with a soapy finger as he stood up.

"Thank you, Daddy," I said automatically, but I was far more focused on the bubbles.

"You're very welcome. Have fun, I'm right here if you need me."

Time was lost to me. Eventually, the bubbles started to dissipate and Daddy appeared by my side as I tried to wrangle as many of the remaining bubbles as I could.

"It's time to put the cup back and get washed," Daddy told me.

"But, Daddy, more bubbles?" I was having fun and didn't want to stop—even if the water was getting a little cold.

"I know, buddy, but the bubbles are almost gone. It's getting late. We'll get you washed and dressed, then you need to clean up your coloring stuff. When that's all done, we can watch another show before bed."

I was going to pretend I wasn't feeling tired. It had to be late, it'd been late when he'd arrived, but I wasn't ready for the night to be over.

I reluctantly handed over the cup. I may have pouted a bit but huffed out an "Okay."

Daddy lathered a washcloth with a bar of soap and set to work cleaning me. He started with my arms, chest, and back before moving down to my legs and feet. I caught myself laughing and squirming as he washed under my arms and the soles of my feet.

"Sit up, buddy, we need to finish getting you clean."

Could he really mean he was going to wash my dick and my ass?

I froze in fear. I was hard, it was obvious through the bubble-free water, but I had been able to largely ignore it while seated. Sitting up would make it impossible to ignore. *Was it okay to be hard when I was little?* It was a fetish, I knew people found it arousing, but I was still scared.

"It's okay, buddy." Daddy must have picked up on my unease because he was rubbing small circles on my back with his fingers. "There's nothing to be ashamed of. Little boys like bath time. It's okay you're enjoying it."

He hadn't come out and said, *"It's okay that you're hard as a rock and enjoying this,"* but he still managed to set my mind at ease.

I slowly sat up on my knees while trying to ignore the erection sticking out in front of me. I couldn't take my eyes off Daddy's hand as he wrapped the washcloth around my dick to clean me. The touch was more intimate than it was clinical, but it also wasn't meant to further my arousal. How he managed to find that balance was a mystery, but I was thankful he had.

When the rest of my body was clean, it was time to get out of the tub. It was strange standing on a bathmat completely naked while someone else dried me. I kept wanting to help and had to remind myself that letting my Daddy take care of me was what I was supposed to do.

After the most thorough drying I'd had in years, another dry, fluffy towel was wrapped around me. "Time to go get your pajamas on," Daddy announced.

Once in the bedroom, Daddy pointed to the small suitcase by the bed. "Are your PJs in there?"

I nodded while noticing I was bouncing slightly. I didn't know if it was from excitement or trying to keep the chill of the air from getting to me.

"Do you mind if I get them for you?"

I shook my head and waited for him to find the clothes. I was nervous about Daddy seeing my pajamas because they definitely didn't look like ones an adult would wear. My pajamas had always been more childish. I liked nostalgic patterns and prints. I could have started buying flannel pajama pants like my older brother wore, or the softer microfiber ones my younger brother preferred, but I just couldn't bring myself to do it.

I was beginning to figure out it was because I liked having a connection to a simpler time in my life.

I'd tossed a blue t-shirt with a large superhero face on it and sleep pants covered with logos from most of my favorite superheroes into my overnight bag. At least they were appropriate for the situation.

"Okay, buddy. Time to get dressed." Daddy placed the folded pajamas on the bed before he reached for the towel wrapped around my waist. I watched as the towel fell away and left me completely exposed. I felt far more vulnerable than I had in the bathroom.

At least the cold air and nerves had fixed the erection

I'd been sporting. Daddy didn't comment on it as he dropped to his knees in front of me and held out the pants.

"Hold onto my shoulders so you don't fall," he instructed after I wobbled slightly trying to feed my leg into the pant leg. Placing my hands on his shoulders to steady myself should have felt strange. It should have made me feel embarrassed. I didn't feel either of those things, though. No, I felt cared for and protected as I used him for balance while he pulled my pants over my feet.

When the vibrant blue cotton pants were over my thighs and butt and situated on my hips, Daddy finally stood up and grabbed the t-shirt off the bed. It was just as bright as the pants and I caught myself grinning as it was pulled over my head. I fed my arms into each armhole before Daddy pulled it down over my stomach.

"Let's go clean up your paper and pencils, then we can watch another cartoon before bed."

If I had been in the room alone, I would have left my drawing stuff out, but for Daddy, I was moving toward the living room without thinking twice. I noticed he didn't let me out of his sight, following me to the living room and watching patiently as I gathered my stuff and took it back to my room.

Since I went through the effort of cleaning up my stuff, I figured I should put it away as well. I scanned the room quickly and found my backpack by the foot of the bed. I tossed it onto the mattress and opened it up to slip my stuff inside.

As I pushed my sketchbook in, I remembered my blanket was inside the bag and I reached for it to give it a squeeze. It was automatic to me—see blanket, touch blanket. The feel of the cool fabric after sitting all day, the texture of the gauze, worn thin by time, soothed me each time I had it in my hands.

I hadn't thought much about it when I packed it before I left home. It had always been nearby. Not always in my bed, but if I wasn't feeling well, was nervous, or even scared, I knew it was just a few steps away. Leaving it at home hadn't even crossed my mind. I'd never gone more than a week or two without it. With Hometown growing more in popularity each week and more commitments being added to my calendar just as quickly, I found myself looking for it before bed more nights than not, which was why it was in my bag in the first place.

Much like my thumb sucking, my older brother teased me mercilessly about my blanket until I got better at hiding it. *When I went to college.* Once I learned to hide it, the habit of touching it when I could became second nature to me.

Even though I was allowing myself to regress slightly around Colt that night, I didn't want him to see my blanket any more than I wanted my brother to see it. In my mind, it was one thing to know the guy you are with is enjoying being little, it was something else entirely to know he still had his original, real-life security blanket.

It hadn't been the sky blue color it once was for more years than I could remember. There was a tear up the center my mom had patched for me when I was in high school after Jasper had tried pulling it from my hand one afternoon. I got a bowl of ice cream while Mom fixed it, and Jasper had been sent to his room. There was a corner missing from when I accidentally shut it in the car door when I was five—by the time we got to my grandparents' house, it was beyond repair and my grandma trimmed it up and hemmed the new corner so it didn't continue to fray.

All of its imperfections made it even more perfect to me.

Apparently, I hadn't been as stealthy as I'd thought when I let my fingers squeeze my blanket because I didn't even have my bag zipped up all the way before Daddy stopped me. "Wait, buddy. Do you have something special in there?"

The red blush that spread across my face gave him the answer immediately. He raised his eyebrows knowingly. "Are you hiding something from Daddy?"

I sucked my lip back into my mouth and worried at it with my top teeth. I realized what I was doing when his hand raised toward me and I released my lip before he could reach it. Met with my silence, Daddy gave me a sympathetic look. "Let's go to the living room and talk."

I watched in horror as Daddy hooked the handle of my backpack and lifted it before taking my hand with his other. As soon as he grabbed the bag, I knew the game was up. He was also looking incredibly Daddy-like. The stern expression on his face was sexy, yet having it directed at me made me want to squirm in my spot. When he started walking, I had no choice but to follow, though I did so hesitantly.

CHAPTER 12

COLT

I WANTED TO KNOW WHO HAD MADE THIS SWEET BOY so ashamed of the item he was scared to even admit to having it. I'd never had felt such a strong urge to protect someone and certainly not after only a day.

Once I set the bag in the center of the couch, I sat down near it and tugged Derek down to me. His butt was situated between my thigh and the arm of the couch and his legs were draped over my lap. "Talk to me, buddy. What has you so worked up?"

I wasn't going to let him get away with silence. The item in the bag was clearly important to him and I had a pretty good idea of what it was. Admittedly, it had taken me longer than it should have to figure it out. At first, I noticed that his hand gripped onto something and I'd assumed he was making space for his drawing stuff. I became confused when I caught a glimpse of the bluish colored fabric. The way he pushed it back and tucked it behind the book finally made it click that he was trying to hide it. From what little I'd seen of it, I suspected it was an old blanket. My heart went out to him—he was outwardly trying so hard to be what everyone else wanted and expected. Privately, he needed to let go yet had no way to do it on his own.

Derek shook his head emphatically, "No, Daddy."

I paused. He was practically vibrating with nerves on my lap. I didn't know him well enough to push him past his comfort zone. "Yellow," I said instinctively. While a sub was most likely to use a safeword, sometimes, Doms needed them too. We needed to talk about this before we moved forward.

Derek's eyes popped open in surprise and he looked at me.

"Sorry, I don't want to alarm you, but we need to talk about this. You're clearly distressed and I'm not going to push you too far."

Derek shook his head. "It's not too far. It's just...personal. I-I don't talk about it."

"That 'no' was strong enough that I need to know—was that a 'no' as in this is a hard limit for you, or was that a 'no' as in you're uncomfortable but need a little push?"

"The second," he admitted as he buried his face into my shoulder.

I wrapped my arms around him and let him lay there for a few minutes before finally speaking. "If I open your bag, are you going to be upset?"

He shrugged. "I don't know, Daddy." He sounded defeated and lost. Frustration laced his voice, but he was done talking and I needed to get back into my Daddy mindset.

I adjusted us slightly so I could see his face more clearly. "Do you have something special in there?" I hedged gently.

He nodded.

"Is there a chicken in there?" I asked, trying to sound far more shocked than amused.

The question took him by surprise and his head shot up as he shook his head rapidly. "No, Daddy!"

"Hmm," I thought, tapping my chin with my finger. "Oh, I know! It's a cheese hat!"

Derek laughed even harder at the ridiculous suggestion, but I was happy I'd helped him forget about his insecurities for a moment. "No, Daddy! It's just my blanket!" His eyes went wide and he clamped his hands over his mouth.

I nodded. I wasn't going to pretend I was surprised by the admission, because I wasn't. "Okay, so now that we've let the big scary secret out, can I open your bag and give you your blanket? Then we can, finally, watch a cartoon."

He nodded slowly, so I reached over and hooked the bag with my index finger. Setting it on his lap, I used the hand that was holding him to my chest to steady the bag while I unzipped it with the other. As soon as the front flopped forward, his blanket was in full view.

Derek reached into the backpack and picked it up, quickly bringing it up so it covered his shoulder. When he was comfortable, he snuggled tightly into my side and stared at the TV.

I wasn't going to make a big deal out of his blanket. He was clearly uncomfortable with how much it meant to him, and I didn't want to ruin his night by pushing him even further. I reached over and grabbed the remote. "Cartoons?"

"Please." His eyes were heavy, but he was fighting sleep with all he had as we found a new superhero show to watch.

I couldn't help but smile down at him. He was going to be trouble when he found his forever Daddy. I ignored the little pang of jealousy I had for the hypothetical man I would never know.

My sweet boy was spent. It was after two in the morning, we'd been up late the night before, he'd had a concert earlier in the evening, and then a big night afterward. It wasn't surprising that as soon as he had his blanket in his hand he'd started to settle down. I knew Derek wasn't going to be long for the world once we turned on the cartoon. His breathing evened out soon after finding the show and he hadn't moved or made a sound in almost fifteen minutes when the closing credits scrolled across the screen.

I hit the power button on the remote and let the room go silent. The only light came from behind us in the kitchen. I took a moment to sit and enjoy the feel of Derek pressed tightly against my chest, his fist resting gently beside his face and his soft breathing filling the silence.

As I placed my hand on his shoulder to wake him, the blanket that had been covering his shoulder and part of his face fluttered down to my lap. Derek had fallen asleep with his right thumb firmly in his mouth. I couldn't decide if I was surprised or not. Earlier in the night, I could have sworn I had seen his thumb move toward his mouth as he thought, but it was so subtle I had just brushed it off as an awkward movement.

Most littles I knew found comfort in the rhythmic sucking of a pacifier. Thumb sucking was basically the same thing, at least in my mind. Hell, at least he wouldn't ever have to worry about losing his favorite paci.

I gave him a gentle squeeze. I wished I could have more time with him to give him all the comfort and love he needed. There was so much about him I didn't know, and I was drawn to him like a moth to a flame.

"Hey, buddy," I coaxed gently. "It's time to tuck you in."

It took a minute for him to stir. "But I want to watch cartoons, Daddy," he mumbled.

I smiled. "Maybe tomorrow. Right now, you need to sleep."

He finally opened his eyes and looked up at me. "You too, right?"

"Yes, me too." I just didn't know where I would be sleeping. I wasn't going to assume he would want me in his bed, but I also didn't want to leave while he wasn't in his normal headspace. Since we had never played like this before, I had no way to judge how far he'd sunk into little space. I also had no idea what type of aftercare he'd need. Just because we hadn't done anything physically taxing didn't mean he wouldn't need it as he came back to himself.

I'd never left a boy without aftercare and I didn't plan to start now.

Derek nodded sleepily and slipped off my lap, heading directly to his room. I pulled the covers back for him, made sure he still had his blanket, and tucked him in. "Sleep well, buddy," I whispered, kissing the top of his head.

He patted the spot beside him in the bed. "Sleep, Daddy."

"With you?"

Derek nodded. "Night," he mumbled as he drifted back to sleep.

I stripped down to my boxer briefs and climbed into the empty side of the bed. I had barely settled in when Derek rolled over and snuggled close. It was a lot like sleeping with a koala, but he had no interest in being anywhere but attached to me.

CHAPTER 13

DEREK

As my brain cleared the fog of sleep from it, I was shocked to find my head was not on a soft pillow but on a firm chest that was rising and falling steadily. Memories of the night before flooded back to me. I didn't even have to look at Colt and I could feel my face heating up.

For a few hours, I had let every worry and stress go. I got to enjoy bath time and snuggle time and I had been able to cuddle without any judgment. He'd even let me watch my favorite cartoon without questioning why I knew the show. Having a Daddy with me had been better than anything my limited fantasies could have conjured up.

I'd been comfortable and warm and Daddy was making sure I was safe. It felt so good to have someone in the room that wasn't one of my bandmates, my manager, or Madeline. Someone who didn't expect me to be Derek Edwards. Someone whose primary focus on making me comfortable and happy, not making me—and often times themselves—more money. But in the light of day, *literally*, I was embarrassed.

My blanket tickled the underside of my nose and I wiggled it. Only then did I notice my thumb was in my mouth. *Fuck*, no matter how relaxing it was, that was a habit I didn't want to pick back up. My personal shit was getting more and more convoluted as the hours passed. I could just see me meeting someone new and trying to explain all of this. *"I'm a submissive, I prefer to bottom, I really want to be Daddy's boy, and I suck my thumb."* They'd go running for the hills.

Yup, I was never going on another date again.

Yet, I had this dream man asleep in my bed who had accepted everything I threw at him without so much as a blink of an eye. He didn't seem to care that I was famous, or hesitant, he just wanted to wrap me up and snuggle away all my uncertainty. But he would be gone in a few hours and I'd be on my way to Memphis.

All good things must come to an end.

Tears were beginning to prick the back of my eyes and I needed to stop letting myself go down this path before I ended the most perfect... date?... two-night-stand?... hook-up?... on a sour note.

Pancakes and bacon sounded like the best way to start the day. I wondered what Daddy—*Colt*, he needed to be Colt now—liked for breakfast. I moved to get up to order room service, but even in his sleep, Colt's arm tightened protectively around me. That small gesture stopped me in my tracks. If he wanted to cuddle for a few more minutes, I wasn't going to stop him. I did have to stop thinking about him as *Daddy*, though, or it was going to be impossible to let him leave.

Curling back into his side, I let myself think about the night before. I kept coming back to the fact that I'd loved every bit of it. If we had more time, I'd have liked to explore the lifestyle further. If anything, I was disappointed our time was coming to an end.

I'd read about submissives hitting subspace, but I'd never experienced anything like it before. Usually, my brain was going a million miles an hour. I would be thinking about the next tour stop, the next meeting, the next interview, the next album. You name it, it was always churning through my brain. As soon as it processed that I had a Daddy that was there to take care of me, the only thing that mattered was my drawing and bath time.

The last bath I'd taken had probably been fifteen, or more, years earlier and I'd likely been sharing the tub with Ty. Having someone—*Daddy*—with me who was in charge of making sure I was clean and wasn't getting cold, allowed me to disconnect and enjoy playing with the bubbles. There was a part of me that thought I should have felt ridiculous, but the rest of me was screaming to let someone take care of me. I didn't want to make decisions, I didn't want to think about my adult life anymore.

When Colt turned into Daddy, everything about it had been hot. I hadn't seen it that way while I was his boy because even knowing how hard I was and how turned on I was, the last thing on my mind was release. Looking back on it, it had been exactly what I needed. However, I hadn't gotten off last night and the thought of how sexy Colt had been had blood rushing south, filling my cock in record time. Sure, I'd woken up with morning wood, but nothing like what it had turned into while thinking about my sexy Daddy.

No, not my *Daddy.*

Inadvertently, I thrust against Colt's thigh which triggered a low groan from his chest. "Good morning," he said, his voice still gravelly from sleep.

"Morning." I pushed my erection back into his hip. The sheet was tented at Colt's waist, encouraging me to go after what I wanted.

I tilted my head up so my lips were near his and went in for a kiss. He met me halfway. The gentle brush of our lips quickly turned deeper.

"What do you need this morning?" Colt asked when our lips parted.

I let out a moan and thrust my hips forward. "I-I need..." Colt reached out and flicked the sensitive bud of my already hard nipple. I whimpered and my breathing became ragged. "Please, please." Suddenly, I knew what I wanted. "I want to ride you," I begged as I began tugging his underwear down.

Colt groaned at my request and shifted slightly, allowing me to pull his underwear off. "My pants. There's lube and a condom." He rolled over to grab the pants he'd shed the night before.

I couldn't help running my dick into the crease of his bare ass. Colt moaned and his head hung off the side of the bed, all of the muscles in his body seemed to give out on him. It was heady to know I had that much power over

Daddy. I silently chastised myself for continuing to think of him like that.

"If you want to ride me, you better not make me cum first," he warned with a hint of playfulness in his voice.

As soon as I saw the foil lube packet in Colt's hand, I reached for it. I had it opened and was squeezing lube onto my fingers before Colt was completely back on the bed.

Reaching behind me, I sunk two fingers deep into my ass. I let out a breathy whimper at the breach, my eyes closing and my head falling back. The groan from Colt was far more audible and I opened my eyes mid-thrust to see him watching me, a hungry glint in his eyes. Oh, he wanted my ass. I forced myself to scissor my fingers to help prepare me a little more for Colt's thick cock, but I didn't have much patience for anything more.

"Condom. Please." I wasn't even on him yet and I was almost a bumbling mess struggling to string a coherent sentence together.

Colt ripped the condom wrapper open and rolled it on.

As my fingers left my ass, Colt reached between my legs, gathering a bit of the extra lube, and proceeded to slick up the condom some more.

So. Fucking. Hot.

I straddled his waist, reaching behind me to guide his dick to my entrance. Sinking back, I took his length in one long, fluid motion. I rested on his thighs for a moment, letting my body adjust to the fullness. I slowly rose up his length before coming down quicker and shivered as his tip hit my prostate in the perfect spot.

Colt reached out, gripping my hips hard enough I

would probably have bruises the next day, but I didn't care. I was going to enjoy the reminder of our time together while they lasted.

I felt sweat gathering on my forehead as I worked. My legs were wearing out but I could feel my orgasm building.

Our combined moans and grunts filled the room as well as the faint smell of arousal. I was babbling nonsensical words of encouragement and praise. Practically chanting, I was begging for everything he could give me. "*More. God. Yes,*" I was rambling as his hips began rising to meet my thrusts.

The sound of skin slapping against skin was enough to drown out some of our groans.

Colt smacked my ass and the sting went straight to my dick causing precum to leak from my tip and fall onto his stomach. "Fuck, yes, harder," I begged. I had never been spanked in the middle of sex, but I needed it right then.

Another crack landed on my other cheek and my toes curled. I rocked my hips slightly forward, causing Colt's dick to nail my prostate at the same time the third spank landed firmly on my ass. I screamed as my orgasm ripped through me and thick ropes of cum shot from my dick, painting Colt's chest and abs.

As the last waves of my orgasm coursed through me, Colt stilled and threw his head back, letting out a deep, almost primal moan as his dick pulsated in my ass. I didn't even have time to collapse on top of him when I heard a familiar voice.

"Shit! Sorry!" Madeline gasped from the doorway. I

turned my head to see her brown ponytail fleeing down the short hallway before the door to the room slammed shut.

"Ugh," I groaned, finally collapsing on Colt's chest.

"Um, who was that?" Colt hedged.

I couldn't help but chuckle at the situation. "That was my personal assistant, Madeline."

"Does she not know how to knock?" Colt finally began to laugh.

I shook my head. "Nope, she's got a key to my room and comes and goes as she pleases."

"Well, this may change that policy."

I hummed my agreement. *I needed to flip the privacy lock every night.* My eyes were beginning to get heavy and I wanted to roll over and go back to sleep. I may have drifted off for a minute when I felt a pop to my backside. "Don't fall asleep on me, there's cum drying between us. If you don't get up, we're going to be stuck together."

"I fail to see the problem," I mumbled.

Another firm slap on my ass and Colt got his sexy Daddy voice out. "You will when our chests are stuck together. Bathroom, now. Then breakfast after."

CHAPTER 14

COLT

"Where are you off to next?" I asked while we each ate a stack of pancakes room service had delivered while we were getting dressed. I had to rewear the same clothes as the night before, but it was worth it to have spent the night with Derek.

Derek shrugged, pushing a bite of pancake around in the puddle of syrup on the corner of his plate.

I wished I had a divided plate and that I could have cut the pancakes up for him before he started eating. Pancakes were a perfect meal for a little boy. Everything from the way he made sure to wash himself in the shower to the way he purposely grabbed his plate of food as soon as we were in the kitchen, told me he didn't want me to be Daddy this morning. Though, the curious glances he shot me from time to time—almost questioning if I was going to stop him from doing something himself—made me think he wouldn't have minded being my boy a little longer.

"We've got two more weeks of touring then we'll get a

'break,'" he used air quotes around the last word, "for a week. I'll be here the entire time. There are a few days of meetings and a few more that will probably end up with us in the studio. I'm honestly not looking forward to it much."

If Derek was going to be back in Tennessee for a week, would he want to meet up again? I certainly wouldn't mind. Just one night of being his Daddy had me wishing for more. I was feeling more protective of Derek than I had of any other little I'd played with. There was part of him just begging to be cared for.

I nodded in response to his admission and tried to sound casual. "Give me a call if you want a break, you're welcome to come out my way for a little bit."

Derek's eyes sparkled. "Thank you."

I didn't want to leave right away, and Derek clearly wasn't itching for me to go either. He took his time eating breakfast. By ten, we could no longer avoid it. Derek's phone had been buzzing consistently for the past thirty minutes—his band was anxious to get on the road to Memphis and his PA was threatening him with bodily harm if he didn't get moving soon.

As I was heading toward the door, there was a sharp knock. Derek tilted his head upward and gave me a chaste kiss. "It's okay if I call you?" he asked as he pulled back.

I nodded. "Anytime. If I don't answer, it's probably because I'm at work. But you can text me any hour of the day."

If Derek's eyes got a little watery, I was going to pretend I hadn't seen it. It would have been far too easy to throw my responsibilities out the window to see where this thing could go between us.

"Thank you for last night," Derek whispered reaching out for the doorknob as another sharp knock shook the door.

He sighed and opened it.

"Derek Edward Scott!" a little brunette scolded as soon as the door opened. The woman, who only came to my chest, was wearing navy blue shoes with short heels and a red sweater dress. "I am so going to kill y-" her lecture died in her throat as I stepped around Derek and leaned down to give him a kiss.

"Have a good day, Derek."

Derek flushed. "You too, Colt."

I walked to the elevator with her voice to my back. "Oh my god, you dog! He's the same guy from two nights ago, isn't he? Holy shit, he's hot!" she was whispering, but her voice echoed down the hallway.

"I'm glad you approve," I called down the hall as I entered the small elevator. As the doors closed, I caught a glimpse of her face. Her mouth was hanging open and there was a bright blush on her cheeks.

Derek was standing in the doorway behind her, stifling a laugh.

At 2:30 on Tuesday afternoon, my phone rang. Derek's picture popped up on the screen and I smiled. After our second night together, I'd set the only picture of Derek I had—the one of him on stage at the Hometown concert—as his contact picture. I smiled every time he called and I got to see his smiling face. I hadn't been up long since I had gotten home after eight that morning and I had slept like the dead until almost three.

"Hey, Derek," I answered as I finished making a sandwich.

My greeting was answered with a yawn on the other end of the line. "Sorry, hey," he mumbled.

Was the mumble just normal tiredness, or was he sitting on the bus with his blanket at his face? Did he want his thumb in his mouth? I didn't feel right asking, but I was going to try to tease out what was making him so tired.

"What are you doing?"

Derek sighed. "Sitting in my dressing room in St. Louis. I think I could sleep for the next week." He yawned again.

"Didn't you sleep well?" I ventured.

"Not nearly well enough. It was seven when we got here and our manager was on the bus immediately chewing me out for having you in my room."

I blinked. "Why? How did he even find out?" I was frustrated with his PA if she had opened her mouth about our time together.

I could almost hear the resigned sigh in his voice. "I told Harrison about you. Not the kinky stuff," he added quickly. "Just the fact that I finally got some, two nights in a row. He's one of my best friends. John overheard, apparently."

"So? Why would John have a problem with that?"

There was a long pause on the other end. If it weren't for the fact that I could hear a commotion in the distance, I would have thought our connection had dropped. "I think it's just hard for him to get used to the fact that I'm gay. He's kind of an old stuffy conservative."

I didn't like the way that sounded. It sounded way too close to, *he's a homophobic asshole* for my liking. I didn't know him, but I didn't like to think that Derek may have his career at the hands of a homophobe.

"It's just been a long day," Derek finished. I could hear his desire to let some of the stress go.

I decided to see how willing Derek would be to give up some control. To see if that would help him find some sense of calm. "When do you have to be onstage?"

"Nothing planned until soundcheck at 5:30."

I looked at the microwave clock. He had just under three hours before he was scheduled to do anything. I thought about it for a few seconds. I didn't have long to make this decision so I was going to have to go with my gut. "Do you have your backpack with you?" I questioned.

Derek hesitated a second, "Yeah."

"Do you still have your blanket in there?"

"Uh... Yes..." he responded hesitantly. I was pretty sure he had probably been chewing on his lip before answering me.

"Great. You need sleep. You're so tired I can hear you drifting off as we talk. Take a minute, text Madeline and tell her you're going to get some rest. Let her figure out what to tell everyone who wants you for anything until at least 4:30."

"Nap time?"

"Yeah, buddy. Little boys need nap time so they can have fun later. Tell Madeline you're done for the next few hours. Get your blanket and go to sleep."

Derek giggled. "Well, I can't disobey Daddy. Okay, I'll take a nap. Can I tell Madeline it is on Daddy's orders?" he joked.

"You tell her whatever you want, but you need sleep now. Goodnight, buddy. Have a good nap."

"Night, Daddy." Derek may have been teasing, but when he called me Daddy, my chest tightened slightly.

After Derek hung up, I set my phone down and grabbed my laptop. Derek was going to be in Tennessee in a few weeks, and he would probably want and need some time to be little. Since I had only played at clubs before, I didn't have nearly enough at home for a little boy.

Two hours later, I was still sitting at my table and had been looking at various adult diaper sites for far too long. I couldn't decide if Derek would want diapers or not. He'd enjoyed being my boy for the night, and his thumb slipping into his mouth at the end of the night was one of the sweetest things I had seen. If he was scared about showing me his blanket, I couldn't imagine him being open about his thumb sucking with anyone else.

He liked being little, he lit up when I put his pajamas on him and he loved the cartoon we found. But, could he see himself in a cute pair of pajamas with a thick diaper between his legs? How much regression would be too much for him?

I caught myself worrying my bottom lip with my teeth

CHAPTER 15

DEREK

Colt: GOODNIGHT. *I'M GOING TO MISS TALKING TO YOU tonight. I have to be at work at 6. Make sure to eat a good breakfast in the morning, it will give you energy for the concert tomorrow evening. Text me when you wake up.*

I grinned. It sounded a lot like, *Eat a good breakfast, you're a growing boy.*

Me: *Oreo O's are a good breakfast, right? Night!*

Brat? Who me? That didn't change the fact that what I really wanted to do was include a *Daddy* after I told him goodnight.

I collapsed back on my bed. Nights on the bus seemed to be getting longer and lonelier. When we did our first tour stint and were just an opening act, the record label had set the entire band up on one tour bus. We would get off stage and all climb onto the bus and talk and laugh until we finally fell asleep. Since we started headlining, there was a small convoy of tour buses.

I was supposed to be sharing a bus with Harrison, but

he left the bus a month earlier saying he was going to hang out with one of our backup musicians. I had a feeling there was something going on between the two of them, but I hadn't pushed, just like he hadn't pushed about what was going on with Colt and me.

It was probably a good thing Harrison hadn't pushed because I was close to spilling. The more we talked on the phone, the more we video chatted, the more I liked Colt. It wasn't like I had a lot of freedom to hook-up with anyone, Colt had been my first and only on tour. Before him, though, I had caught glimpses of men in the crowd and there had been a few local sound guys who had given me a lingering glance who I'd thought were cute. But, I hadn't even noticed another man since I'd met Colt. There hadn't been a single person my eyes lingered on for a few seconds too long, or my dick took interest in. Though, every time I saw Colt's picture on my phone or laptop screen, my dick was completely interested.

It had been ten days since we left Nashville and we'd be returning in four. We would be in Cleveland for a show that night, then Columbus, and finally Lexington. We'd have a night of travel and then we would arrive in Nashville. The last few days of the trip were turning out to be hell.

We'd left Chicago later than we normally did thanks to backstage delays and drove through the night to get to Cleveland. I usually slept like the dead on the bus, but we'd driven through a nasty snowstorm that started just outside of Chicago and the buses hadn't been able to go a continuous speed after. We'd fishtailed, sped up, and slowed down depending on the conditions, and I had never been able to fall into a good sleep. By the time we made it to the Ohio border, the snow had slowed up and dawn was beginning to show on the horizon.

At 5:30 a.m. I gave up on sleep. I found my favorite channel on the TV to watch the morning cartoons. I was also thankful I'd asked Madeline to run out and get me crayons one night while we were on stage. She hadn't just bought me crayons either. When I'd climbed onto the bus, I'd found the deluxe box of crayons and a stack of coloring books on my table. The top two were adult coloring books, but the bottom two were for children—one with cars, trucks, and trains, and one with animals. It made me wonder what she knew, but I wasn't about to ask her.

As I concentrated on coloring the picture of a cheetah, the occasional bumps of the highway making me color outside of the lines slightly, I decided I wanted to give my picture to Daddy. I had worked so hard to not think about Colt as Daddy, but each time we talked, each time we texted, that line between the strong, assertive Sheriff West-field, and the tender, caring Daddy got blurred a little more in my mind.

I spent my time not sleeping, coloring a picture for Daddy. I needed to face the fact that I liked Colt being my Daddy. I liked when he got growly and told me to take better care of myself. I wanted to please him. I wanted to see him smile when I gave him a picture I worked hard to color for him. I hoped he'd understand just how special my picture was—the first picture I had ever colored for my Daddy.

Why did that thought make my chest feel so tight?

I was still splitting my time between coloring and watching the superhero show when my phone buzzed at 6:45. We were finally in Toledo and had a little over an hour before we'd reach Cleveland.

Colt: *Oreo O's do not count as a good breakfast. Make sure to get protein. If you have to, ask Madeline to order you something, but you have oatmeal with granola on the bus, that would be a good filling breakfast. I am going to be disappointed if I find out you ate that crap cereal instead.*

Well fuck, why did he have to sound so reasonable? And why did he have to sound so much like my dream Daddy? My brain focused in on the word disappointed and my attempts at brattiness were gone. I wanted to please him. It didn't matter if he was Colt or Daddy, I wanted him to be proud of me.

Me: *Alright, I'll be good. Oatmeal and granola. Can I at least put brown sugar in it?*

The response was almost instant.

Colt: *What are you doing up so early? Only a spoonful of sugar. It's not good to start your morning with a bunch of sweet stuff.*

Me: *Long night :'(Lots of snow, rough going, didn't sleep much. We're in Ohio now, the snow stopped, but now the sun is coming up and I can't sleep. I'll be good, not too much sugar, promise.*

Colt: *Sorry you didn't get sleep. Try to get a nap today if you can. You need more sleep than you've been getting.*

Me: *I can sleep when I'm dead.*

Unfortunately, if I didn't start getting more sleep than I

had been, I may end up dying earlier than I wanted. The lack of sleep was starting to catch up with me.

Colt: *More sleep, no death. Got a call. Talk later.*

I sighed and tried to finish my picture, but my heart wasn't in it anymore. It was late enough in the morning I could justify eating breakfast. Setting my blanket and coloring stuff aside, I headed to the small kitchen to make oatmeal. Even if Colt would never know I had Oreo O's instead of oatmeal, I told him I'd have oatmeal and I'd feel guilty if I didn't.

I suffered through my oatmeal—even adding a side of plain Greek yogurt for the protein he told me I needed—while staring at the cabinet that held the sweet cereal that I had teased Daddy about. It was getting way too easy to think of him as Daddy, especially when I was tired.

Twenty minutes after finishing my breakfast, I headed back to my bunk hoping I could maybe get some sleep. I climbed into the bed and closed my eyes when I had my blanket in my hand. The last thought I had was if Colt would mind if I came to visit when we got to Nashville later in the week.

"Derek!" Madeline was shaking my shoulder what felt like ten seconds after I laid down. Then I heard her laughing. "You and that damn blanket."

I cracked an eye open. "Sleep," I mumbled only to feel my thumb in my mouth. *Shit.* It was finding its way there with more frequency. After being aggravated with myself for beginning to suck it again, I was finding comfort in it. There was something soothing about waking up sucking my thumb. I'd actually caught myself trying to let it slip in a few times after concerts when I was getting tired.

I pulled my thumb out as discreetly as possible and rolled over to look at Madeline. "What?"

"You are late for that radio interview. You're supposed to be in the studio in twenty minutes, we've been calling and texting you for half an hour!"

I must have been really out of it to not hear my phone. But I jumped out of bed and hurried through my routine. I'd only gotten two hours of sleep, but it would have to do until after the concert that night.

The rest of the day went much the same as the morning. I was exhausted before stepping onto the stage. By the time we sang the finale, Harrison was starting to shoot me questioning glances.

"You okay?" he asked, as I headed toward my dressing room.

"Tired. I'll be fine, I just need some sleep."

He looked at me skeptically. "When was the last time you got a good night's sleep?"

Did I want to tell him the last time I slept a full night was when Colt was in my bed? I had just gotten over the teasing from Madeline walking in on us having sex. "It's been a few weeks now, I think. I'm looking forward to being in Nashville for a week."

"Do you still have the contact info for tall, dark, and sexy?" Harrison asked quietly.

I almost tripped over my feet. "What? Why?"

"Um, because he fucked you into oblivion and you were riding high for days afterward. I think you need more of that. Maybe after a round between the sheets, you'll actually sleep for more than a few hours."

I rolled my eyes and pushed his shoulder. "Go get showered. We have to be loaded up in an hour."

If he only knew how much I needed Daddy right then he would probably laugh at me.

CHAPTER 16

COLT

It was unreasonable to be as concerned about Derek as I was. We weren't even, technically, dating. The last three nights had seen him getting more and more exhausted. I was actually worried about him being able to perform at the Lexington show. He was so rundown when we talked that morning he'd just sat on his bed and barely talked to me between jaw-popping yawns.

Telling me he wasn't sleeping well was not helping my frustration. If I could figure out what asshole scheduled four tour stops in a row in three different states, I would've given them a piece of my mind.

When Derek's thumb finally made its way to his mouth, I knew my boy was spent. He was on his last reserves and he had to be on stage in less than an hour.

"You'll be in Tennessee tomorrow, buddy," I told him as I pushed a drawer in my spare room shut with my foot. Derek didn't have a clue that the drawer was filled with new pajamas I had ordered for him, nor did he know that the drawer beside it was filled with diapers.

Derek nodded, not even bothering to take his thumb out of his mouth, his eyes had dark circles under them from lack of sleep, and my chest tightened. He needed a hug, instead he got a barked order, "Get off the bus, now, you're late!" from John.

"I guess I should go," he sighed as he removed his thumb from his mouth and set his blanket on the bed beside him.

"Have a good show," I told him. "Last one for a bit."

He nodded. "Bye, Daddy."

"Bye, buddy." He disconnected the video and I was left wondering if he had even caught his slipup. Derek Edwards was done being *on,* he needed some time to be Derek Scott and not at everyone's beck and call.

We hadn't discussed seeing each other beyond a few conversations in passing, but I was expecting at least a night or two over the next week when Derek would be ready to step away from Nashville. I needed to focus on getting things ready for my boy.

With his clothes and diapers put away, I set to work unpackaging the blocks, cars, trains, and little plastic people I had found at the store earlier that week. It wasn't a lot of toys, but it would give him something to play with while he was here. We could always go get more later.

I had found an entire bedding set of the cartoon with the pajama wearing superheroes Derek liked. After picking up the bedding set, I also bought the plush heroes that went with it. Even if it was only used for nap or play-time, at least Derek had a room just for him in my house.

I was getting ahead of myself. I knew that. Derek deserved to let it all go and I knew I could give him that ability. The real question was, *was Derek going to be on board?* I was going to have to be patient for a few more days at least.

Going to the kitchen, I found space in the cabinet for the divided plate, bottle, and sippy cup I bought him. Not knowing much about Derek's preferences, especially relating to his little side, I tried not to go overboard. I wanted him to have things at my house, but I also wanted him to be able to have a say in it too. If it was something he enjoyed, I wanted him to pick out what he liked most.

I hadn't heard anything from him when I went to bed at eleven and could only hope his night had improved from when I had talked to him earlier. I didn't sleep well knowing Derek was stretched so thin and there was nothing I could do until he reached out to me.

CHAPTER 17

DEREK

Harrison showed up by my bed Monday morning when we pulled into Nashville. I had barely slept, again. My brain hadn't stopped reeling all night. Part of it was that I was stressed about being stressed all the time. The other part of it was that I got off stage in Lexington feeling like we had disappointed the crowd. Every issue had been outside of our control—the venue must have hired kindergartners to do the sound and light rigging for us. Despite sound checks, the sound cut out on us three separate times during our set, and the lighting was sporadic at best.

I had spent an entire song singing in pitch black with my sound cutting in and out. Thankfully, the audience seemed to enjoy themselves, but there would definitely be backlash. The thought that we had disappointed the fans was eating at me.

"You sleep at all?" Harrison questioned as I rolled out of my bed.

I shook my head. "Not much."

"Have you called your man?" he asked me as I was pulling a pair of jeans on over my briefs.

"First, he's not my man. And no." I forced my head through an old red hooded sweatshirt. "I haven't." I didn't care that we were going to be in meetings with the record label all day, I just wanted one day where I could be totally comfortable. I had seriously contemplated wearing my sweatpants instead of jeans.

Harrison crossed his arms over his chest. "Dare, we've been friends for a long time and I'm worried about you. You haven't slept well in weeks. The circles under your eyes have circles at this point.

I clapped him on the shoulder. "Thanks, Harrison. I appreciate your concern and I'll make sure to take some time for me this week. Promise."

Harrison nodded like he was happy with my response, if not totally convinced. "Great, now let's go figure out what's up at the label."

———

NOT EVEN AN HOUR into the first meeting and I wished I had stayed in bed. The head of the record label was in the conference room talking about extending the tour. Judging by the looks on the faces around the room, I wasn't the only one who wasn't on board with the idea. Though Harrison was the first to speak up.

"We just had *four* concerts in a row. Have any of you even *looked* at Derek this week? He looks like death warmed over. He looks like the rest of us feel. By the time this tour wraps up, we are going to have been to *every* state in the US. If we don't hit every large city in the country, I think our fans can wait a year or so."

I nodded dumbly, agreeing with everything Harrison was saying. I was just too overwhelmed to respond at first.

Gina jumped up. "We need to talk about this as a band, after we've all had more than ten hours of sleep in the last four days. You all have said *jump* and we've said *how high* way too many times this tour. We aren't making this decision now."

I listened to the people around me argue for another twenty minutes before I finally stood up. "I can't do this right now," I said as I walked toward the door.

"Derek, wait!" I heard Harrison call behind me as I exited the room. The elevator door slid open to let a group of businessmen off and I walked toward it, letting it shut behind me just as Harrison flung the conference room door open. "DEREK!" he yelled as the doors finally closed.

I pushed the button for the first floor and spent the ride to the ground floor calling a car service from my phone. The ETA was less than two minutes. All I wanted to do was get back to the bus, pack a bag, and call Colt. I needed out.

My phone was blowing up with texts from various band members as well as Madeline. She had planned to meet friends for lunch, but apparently someone had alerted her that I had gone AWOL.

A blue car pulled up as my phone pinged letting me know my driver had arrived. I sighed in relief as I climbed into the car and laid my head back against the headrest. As the car pulled away from the curb, I saw Harrison run out the front door of the building and scan the area looking for me.

I let out an audible sigh, I needed to let someone know I was okay, at least.

Me: *Tell the guys I'm okay. I just... can't do this right now. Too tired. I'll see everyone tomorrow.*

Madeline: *Jesus H Christ, you have them all scared shitless! You sure you're ok?*

Me: *Maddie, I'm fine. I'm tired. I'm stressed. I'm calling Colt and I am going to be gone the rest of the day. I'll be back at 10 tomorrow.*

Madeline: *As far as everyone else is aware, I'm pissed as hell at you for pulling this stunt. Between me and you, I have *no* idea where you are, just that you've assured me you'll be back in the a.m. and you're fine.*

Me: *Thank you!*

By the time I got back to the bus, I was no longer feeling numb. I was, however, beginning to feel like the weight of the world was pressing on my shoulders. I hoped Colt didn't mind that I was going to call him in the middle of the morning.

I collapsed on the couch in my bus as soon as I walked through the door, not even making it to my bed to pack my stuff. I pulled my cell phone out of my pocket and pressed Colt's contact number. It rang twice before he answered.

"Hey! I wasn't expecting to hear from you so early," he said. His voice was smooth, but the happiness I detected in it when he answered my call made the last of my resolve shatter.

"Daddy," I gasped as tears filled my eyes and spilled over.

"Whoa, buddy. What's wrong?" he asked, his cool demeanor changing to concerned in a matter of seconds.

"I-I-I need you," I choked out.

"Where are you? I'll be there as soon as I can."

It dawned on me that he didn't even know if I was in Nashville at that point. He was just ready to drop everything to get to me and that meant more to me than I could put into words. Colt had become my Daddy without me realizing it. I'd read that when it came to BDSM, relationships developed far faster. I just never expected to find someone who would be willing to drop everything to get to me after having only known me for a few weeks.

"O-okay," I sniffled. "I'm on the outskirts of downtown Nashville. I'll text you the address."

"Alright, buddy. I need to get my shoes on. As soon as your text comes, I'll be on my way. It'll take me about a half hour or so to get there depending on what part of town you're in."

As soon as we hung up, I texted Daddy my location and turned the screen off. I sniffled and began to pull myself back together. Once I felt like I could function again, I went back to my bunk and began to pack the important things—my blanket, crayons, coloring books, and clothes. I didn't even care if I forgot clothes at that point, honestly.

CHAPTER 18

COLT

My stomach had dropped hearing the little gasp on the other end of the line when Derek called. I knew he had been burning the candle at both ends, but to hear him break down like that was almost too much for me.

I was already in my truck when his text came through. As soon as I put the address in the navigation app on my phone, I was on my way. I had about half an hour before I would get there so I took the time to make a phone call to my deputy.

"Hey, Chief," he answered after two rings. The first two years he worked with me, his nickname for me had driven me nuts. I wasn't a police officer, I was a sheriff. Then I realized he was still calling me Chief *because* it drove me nuts, but by that point it was just habit and I learned to embrace it.

"Hey, Zander, I hate to do this, but I need this week off."

There was silence on the other end, so long that I

checked our connection. "Chief, I've been here three years and I can count on one hand the number of *half* days you've taken. Is everything okay?" he was clearly concerned. I had a well-earned reputation for being a workaholic.

"I'm fine. I just had something come up and I need some time off. I'll be back next week, and I'll give you extra time off the next few weeks to make up for it," I told him.

"Colt," Zander addressed me using my first name, possibly for the first time ever. "We'll see you when you get back. No one needs extra time off. We'll survive."

I sighed. "Thanks, Zander. Call if you need anything, I'll be around."

"Later. Take care of yourself." Zander disconnected and I couldn't help but smile. I was far more concerned about taking care of my boy than my job right then.

Since rush hour was over, the drive didn't even take me the predicted thirty minutes. I was pulling up to a row of buses parked in a lot just north of downtown twenty-six minutes after pulling out of my driveway.

Me: *I'm here, buddy. Which bus are you on?*

Derek: *The last bus in the lot.*

Me: *I'm pulling up now.*

I stopped and headed up to the door of the last bus just as it opened. Derek's eyes got wide, almost like he couldn't believe I was there, before they softened and turned watery. I climbed the steps and made it onto the bus before Derek buried his face in my shoulder and began to cry.

Rubbing soothing circles on his back, I let him cry himself out. By the time he pulled back, his eyes were red-rimmed and puffy but there was a bashful smile on his face. "Sorry, Daddy," he told me, digging at the floor with his big toe.

"Don't be. Do you want to get out of here? Maybe head to my house today?"

Derek nodded vigorously. "Please."

Happy to hear that word, I gave him another squeeze. "Let's get your stuff. We'll be out of here in just a few minutes."

Derek led me to the back of his tour bus. It was nicer than my first three apartments with leather couches in the front, granite countertops in the kitchen and dark mahogany cabinetry and accents throughout the entire bus. As we walked to the back, we passed a small bathroom with a tiled shower before we made it to the bunk area. I found it odd there were enough bunks to sleep the entire band, yet Derek was typically the only one on the bus.

Derek leaned into his bunk and grabbed a suitcase, guitar case, and his backpack. He had been ready to get out of there as quickly as possible. I reached out and took the backpack from him, slinging it over my shoulder and then grabbed the suitcase in my left hand.

"Let's go." I held out my right hand and Derek took it before grabbing his guitar with his free hand and allowing me to lead the way out of the bus. I waited while he locked the door and we walked to my truck in silence. Derek stood with me while I put his suitcase and guitar in the backseat before opening the passenger door for him.

He climbed up without saying a word and I set his backpack between his legs. I wanted him to have easy access to his blanket if he wanted it. Walking around to the driver's side of the truck, I climbed in and looked over at Derek. He hadn't made a move to buckle himself in, so I reached across the cab and grabbed his belt.

"I need my boy to be safe," I told him as I clicked the buckle into place.

Derek hummed softly and nodded. "Thank you, Daddy."

My boy was done, but we needed to talk before he got too deep into his role. I pulled the truck onto the road before I began.

"You were supposed to be in meetings all day. What happened?" I tried to not make my voice too accusatory.

Derek blinked a few times before he turned to me. "They didn't go well. Well, they didn't start well. The higher ups want to add tour dates. Everyone started arguing with each other and I just kind of shut down. I walked out."

"You walked out?" Did that mean out of the meeting or out of the band? Did anyone even know where he was?

I saw Derek nod once. "Of the meeting. I just walked out. I was so tired and the last thing I wanted to do was talk about adding more tour dates. I probably shouldn't have just walked out though, huh?" It was like it just dawned on him what he had done.

"Does anyone know where you are?" I probed gently.

He nodded again. "I told Madeline I was calling you and I'd be back for the next meeting tomorrow. I-I just need time to be me for a little while."

I was going to need to get Madeline's number at some

point. If Derek was going to be spending time with me—especially if he was going to be able to let himself go and be my boy—I needed to make sure he wasn't being bothered by his phone and outside demands. If people continued to call his phone and text, it would pull him out of his role every single time. If Madeline had my number, we could silence his phone and she could contact me with anything important.

Derek's head turned toward me. "I don't want to think anymore. I need sleep, so bad. Do, do you think we could try letting me just be your boy for today? I've never gotten to do that, but it sounds so... nice... relaxing maybe? My brain needs to turn off for a little bit."

Derek sounded desperate for the opportunity. It was what I already had planned, so it was an easy answer for me. "Of course, as soon as we get to my house. Do you know how far you want to go?"

"Uhh..." Derek seemed genuinely confused. "I've never done this. Can you tell me how you'd like to see the day going and I can try to figure it?"

I thought of what would sound most appealing to him and started there.

"Well, I think the first step will be getting you ready for the day. You can choose between pajamas or a play outfit. It should be late enough to eat lunch after that. You'll be able to play with your toys or color while I make lunch. I'll make sure you have a bottle or a sippy cup while you eat. Then after, you're going to need a nap."

Derek laughed. "What exactly do play clothes look like? I haven't had those since I was about eight, and even then they were just my old stained up jeans and t-shirts that my mom didn't care if I got muddy."

I smiled at him. "I'll let you look when we get back. I may have some fun surprises for you."

"A bottle or a sippy cup?" He sounded torn on those items.

I kept my tone casual. "Yes, when your little, your drinks will be in a sippy cup or a bottle. I'll let you choose this time. There will be times Daddy gets to choose depending on what I think you need." I didn't want to overwhelm him with the idea of diapers and naps in his own room so I left those things out.

Out of the corner of my eye, I saw Derek begin to chew on his lip. I was going to have to find something to help him keep his lip out of his mouth. "Honestly, I don't mind any of your ideas for today. But I get the impression you aren't telling me something. If you had your ideal day with me, what would it look like?"

So much for not overwhelming him.

"Remember, we don't have to do this if you're not comfortable with it," I began. "But my perfect day with you would be getting you home and helping you into a thick diaper and play clothes."

I glanced over to see his eyes widen at the mention of diapers but he didn't stop me. He wiggled slightly in his seat and adjusted himself in his jeans, though. He may not have known if he was going to like diapers, but his dick seemed to like the idea just fine. "Then, I'd get you set up with some toys to keep you busy while Daddy makes lunch. I'd make sure to use a kids plate for your lunch and give you a sippy cup of juice."

Derek smiled at that, a clear indication he didn't mind the idea. "After lunch, I'd make you a bottle of milk and take you to your room and tuck you in for naptime."

"Is there a story before nap?" Derek asked. The way his eyes widened in surprise, I figured he hadn't actually meant to ask the question out loud.

"If my boy likes stories, that can certainly be arranged." I was glad I had impulse-bought a few books at the store. Having a small shelf of books seemed necessary when I thought of a room for my boy.

"After naptime, you could play or watch TV until it's time for dinner. Then it would be bathtime and time for bed. Of course, I'd change you anytime you needed it throughout the day."

"Um, I don't know about the diapers," Derek admitted.

"That's okay. They are a big step. You asked what my ideal day with you little would look like, and that would be it. We can work up to diapers. We can even work up to bottles if that feels too big right now."

Derek thought about it for a few seconds. "Diapers are too much for me right now. I don't know that they will always be too much, but right now, yes."

"Thank you for your honest answer. I won't push about them until we've had time to explore more. As your Daddy, I may push sometimes, especially if I think it's something you need."

Derek nodded to himself. "I like the idea of playtime, and naptime." His stomach let out a growl that filled the cab. "And my stomach, especially, likes lunch." He laughed.

I pulled off the main road onto the gravel drive leading to my house. It was a white farmhouse I had purchased five years earlier. The amount of work it needed when it went on the market wasn't my only hesitation about purchasing the home. My parents owned the property next door. But, a dense patch of trees separated our homes and they were over a quarter mile away.

My mom and sister had a tendency to barge into my house unexpectedly which wasn't usually a problem. I would have to remember to lock the doors and pull the curtains now that Derek was at my house. If they caught wind of the fact that I had taken the week off, there would be no keeping them away.

Since buying the house, I had repainted all the clapboard siding, added shutters, repaired and stained the deck boards, and painted the spindles. It had been a labor of love on the outside, but on the inside I had set my mom free. It was probably a weird thing to trust her with, but she had impeccable style and I just didn't care much about it. My mom had had the hardwood floors refinished and had the fireplace restored. She had already ordered the white marbled quartz countertops and white shaker cabinets before I even had a chance to ask what her plans were. My dining room had a modern gas fireplace installed and the table was chunky, reclaimed wood, that sat twelve. It was excessive for a single guy, but my sister and her friends often migrated to my house to escape Mom and Dad and the table was always a good gathering place for them.

"Wow," Derek said, his eyes going wide as we rounded the bend of the driveway, bringing my home into full view. "It's beautiful. My mom would flip for your porch."

"Thank you." I was happy he appreciated it. I hoped he would also feel at home.

I pulled to a stop in front of the garage and got out. "When we get inside, you're just going to be my boy for the day. You already told me you're not comfortable with diapers. Is there anything else I should know before we go inside?"

Derek shook his head. "Traffic light system if I need it, right?" he asked.

"Absolutely. No judgement. If something gets to be too much, tell me your safeword and we'll talk through it or stop completely."

"Then I'm ready."

I smiled. "I'll come around to get you."

Derek sat patiently while I got out and went to his side. I opened the back door and got his suitcase first, then opened his door. I noticed he hadn't unbuckled. I didn't know if it was that he hadn't thought of it, or if he thought it was something Daddy should do. It didn't matter to me either way. I leaned over and unbuckled him. "Come on, we'll get you ready, then you can look to see what you want to play with while I make lunch."

Derek nodded and took my hand as he slid out of the cab. I reached behind him and grabbed his backpack and we headed into the house. The heater had done a nice job keeping up with the early February cold, so it was warm and cozy. I would probably start a fire later in the day if

Derek wanted to play in the living room to keep his legs from getting chilled.

Derek's eyes were wide as we walked through the main level and toward the steps leading upstairs. I walked by the first guest room and my home office to the room I had made up for Derek. It had been a huge gamble but it had already paid off.

CHAPTER 19

DEREK

I FELT LIKE I WAS HAVING AN OUT OF BODY experience. We were talking about wearing—*and potentially using*—diapers. I hadn't worn diapers since I was a toddler and I didn't think I was ready to start again, even if there was a part of me that was curious. Bottles and sippy cups and toys were dancing around my mind. Part of me couldn't believe what I was hearing, not out of shock, but because it all felt so right. I hadn't used any of those items in longer than I could remember, but I wanted them all. *Maybe even the diapers.* I didn't have the words to vocalize my feelings on the subject, but when naptime was brought up, I really hoped that also meant a story.

The thought apparently came out of my mouth, too, because Daddy told me he would read me a book if I wanted one before my nap. The idea of having a bedtime story should have been awkward, but it sounded peaceful. I'd be able to curl up with Daddy and do nothing but soak up all his attention.

I don't know what I expected Colt's house to look like, but the beautifully restored white farmhouse with a wrap-around porch was not it. It was a big house for a single guy, but every part of it seemed to be well-thought-out and executed. As we walked through the living room, toward the stairs, I took in the oversized couches in the living room that looked like they would swallow me up if I sat down, and a spacious kitchen with a huge island that invited guests to sit down. Even the dining room at the far end was welcoming. This was a home for someone with a family and I wondered if that was something he wanted. I didn't have a lot of time to dwell on it though because he was leading me upstairs past an office, a small room, and a few closed doors toward a room at the end of the hall.

As we entered the bedroom, I felt my eyes go wide and my mouth drop open. There was a full-sized bed against the far wall decorated in bedding with characters from my favorite cartoon. On the bed sat a stuffed version of each character just begging to be snuggled. Adult thoughts seemed to drop from my head as I took in the room.

Buckets lined one wall. Each one had a different hand-written label—*Trains, Cars, Blocks, Animals*. A small stack of books sat on a white nightstand beside the bed that also held a lamp with a star-shaped base.

Daddy put my suitcase along the wall by the door and my backpack closer to the nightstand. "Is your blanket in your backpack?"

I nodded as a yawn escaped. The bed looked so inviting, I wanted to crawl into it and go to sleep. I had a feeling

Daddy wouldn't let me sleep unless I had lunch though, and my stomach agreed.

I watched as he knelt down and unzipped my bag, finding my coloring books and crayons before finally pulling my blanket out and handing it to me. "Do you want to color before lunch or do you want to play with toys?"

Coloring or toys? Coloring or toys? It was almost too difficult to decide, but the bucket of trains was calling to me. "I want to play with the trains, Daddy." I was still having a hard time understanding why it was so easy to call Colt *Daddy*, but it felt right.

He seemed perfectly fine with my decision. "Okay, we need to get you ready first, then we'll take the bucket of trains downstairs."

He leaned over and pulled open a drawer under the bed. I looked down to see a few clothing items. They were all either brightly colored shirts, and what looked like matching shorts—loose cotton shorts like I sometimes saw kids wearing. There was a light gray colored something, with blue piping around the edges and patterned with brightly colored fluff-balls with smiling faces. The snaps down the center of it caught my eyes.

Was that an outfit to wear with a diaper?

While I logically knew that diapers were going to be a huge step in our relationship that I wasn't ready to take yet. I had a feeling that I would try them—probably sooner than I was letting myself admit. My dick already liked the idea more than my head and was filling as I stood there. The few times I'd managed to look up age play, I couldn't help but notice how cute the subs looked in their diapers. I wondered if I would look as sweet. It was still hard to see myself as a little when I looked in the mirror and saw a six-foot-tall guy who weighed almost 200 pounds.

Daddy looked up at me and smiled softly. "Arms up so we can get this shirt off."

I raised my arms without hesitation and he pulled both my hoodie and t-shirt off at once. The house was warm, but a shiver ran through my body when the air touched my skin.

"It's okay, we'll get you dressed again in just a minute," Daddy told me as he gathered a bright green t-shirt with the words "Daddy's Boy" across the chest and matching shorts from the drawer. I was bouncing with excitement as soon as I saw it. *I was Daddy's Boy!*

The grin that split Daddy's face was genuine happiness. "I see someone likes his new clothes."

I nodded excitedly. It struck me this was the happiest I had been in weeks, if not months. I hadn't been anywhere near this happy since I'd left Nashville two weeks earlier, I knew that for certain. "I like my shirt, Daddy."

"I'm glad to hear that," he told me as he kissed my forehead. He pushed the drawer closed with his foot. "Okay lay down on the bed, I'll get your blanket and we'll get you dressed."

I sat down on the bed and found the red superhero. I pulled it close to my chest as I waited for Daddy to find my blanket.

This was easy.

I got to lay back and play with toys and my Daddy was going to take care of the rest. He already had taken care of me—new toys, new clothes, and a bed with my favorite cartoon characters. The tears were going to start again soon if I didn't get myself under control. I focused back on what Daddy was doing in time to see him hand over my blanket.

I reached for it and as soon as it was in my hand, my thumb went to my mouth. It didn't matter if I *wanted* to be a thumb sucker again or not, I was going to have to accept it was part of me.

"Lift up for me, buddy," Daddy's voice sounded distant, but I lifted my hips and felt my pants being slid down my legs.

"We're going to have to work on some more appropriate undies for you when you're little. These are very nice briefs for big boys, but when you're little, we need something that looks more the part." Daddy didn't seem to be expecting a reply from me, so I just lay there with my eyes closed.

I heard shuffling and then felt the pants being pulled up my legs. "Up again," Daddy instructed as they reached my thighs. How he avoided brushing my rock hard dick while putting my shorts on was a mystery because I could feel it snaking up toward the waistband of my underwear. It had to have been obvious while putting the shorts on me, but he didn't even seem to notice it.

"Sit up, now. Time for your shirt." He held a hand out for me and I accepted the help up. "Thumb needs to come out for just a minute," Daddy said with a chuckle when the shirt was ready to go over my head. "As soon as you're dressed it can go back in." He tugged gently at my hand

and I let my thumb fall from my mouth. "There you go. Arms up."

Within seconds, my shirt was on. The outfit felt different from anything I could remember wearing. It was childish and bright and made me feel good. I ran my finger over the letters and looked up at Daddy. "Thank you," I managed to get out.

He pulled me into a hug. "You're welcome, buddy. I'm glad you're here."

CHAPTER 20

COLT

I WAS TRYING HARD NOT TO CUT MY FINGERS OFF AS I cut the peanut butter and jelly sandwich into triangles for Derek. He'd been laying on the living room floor for twenty minutes while I made lunch for him. His feet were moving back and forth in the air while he pushed a train around the wooden track he had set up.

As soon as we got to the living room, he'd been ready to play. There wasn't a second of hesitation as he sat down on the floor and began to dig through the bucket. Even I was surprised at how easily he took to it. The added noise of Derek making train sounds, the wooden wheels rolling over the tracks, and the magnets clacking together filled a void in my house I hadn't realized was there.

I finally managed to pull myself back to making lunch. I wasn't much of a fan of peanut butter and jelly sandwiches, so I warmed up some pasta for myself and plated a decent sized salad. With Derek's sandwich made, I was able to focus on pulling grapes off the stems and finding the baby carrots I knew were in the fridge.

I almost let out a whoop when I found the homemade pudding that had been leftover from dinner the night before at my parents' house. My mom had made enough to feed an army and wouldn't let me leave until I had a container of it.

I grabbed one of the divided plates I'd picked out for Derek and plated his lunch. Looking at the dump truck plate, I smiled. The front wheel contained carrots and ranch dip. The rear wheel held grapes and apple slices. The portion for the cab was filled with chocolate pudding and in the bed was his sandwich with cheese cubes to the side. It looked plenty filling and judging by the yawns I was hearing from the living room, I didn't know if he'd be able to eat even half of his meal before he was falling asleep.

Before going to get Derek, I filled his sippy cup with apple juice and placed everything on the island for him. I rarely ate at the dining room table and thought it would be awkward to start now. I pulled a chair to the opposite side of the counter so I could see him while we ate.

"Hey, buddy. It's time to put the trains away so we can have lunch." I crouched down in front of him. "You can play after nap if you have time."

"But trains..." he trailed off into a yawn.

"Hungry and sleepy boys who also want a story before naptime need to get their toys cleaned up."

He sighed but began to put his trains away. When the last one was in the bucket, his stomach growled again.

"Yeah, it's time for lunch. Can we leave your blanket on the couch? I think you'd rather have it in bed with you than in the washer because there's food on it."

Derek looked unconvinced. "I guess. Lunch, then story, then nap? Right?"

I smiled. "Yes. Lunch, story, and nap."

I set the bucket next to his blanket so I would remember to take them both upstairs after lunch, and we headed to the kitchen. There was a pause in Derek's steps when he saw his food cut up and placed on his plate so it didn't touch. His eyes locked onto the yellow sippy cup with an orange lid and he didn't seem to know what to do with it.

After tripping over his tongue for a moment, and starting and stopping a sentence a few times he finally got a full thought out. "It looks good, Daddy. Thank you." I kissed his temple and walked him to his chair. "Sit down and eat. Can you stay clean or do we need to take your clothes off for lunch?" I'd been joking, but if I got Derek some training pants, he would look adorable sitting at the island in only his undies. I tried to discreetly adjust my rapidly growing cock as I walked around the island.

Derek giggled. "I'll be clean, Daddy." He started with the carrot sticks and ranch dressing before going to the fruit. I looked up to find him dipping the grapes into the chocolate pudding. I was slightly offended, but he was eating well so I didn't say anything about it.

By the time the sandwich and cheese were gone, he was giving his sippy cup long contemplative glances. I gave him time to work through his thoughts and eventually he picked it up. Holding it in his hand, he seemed torn between actually taking a drink and putting it down. I didn't know what was going through his head, it almost looked like he was giving himself a mental pep-talk. After another minute I heard him mumble, *fuck it*, and put the cup to his mouth.

I fought hard to keep the smile off my face, choosing instead to take another bite of my pasta. At some point, he'd be reminded about his language while he was little, but now wasn't the time.

A few minutes later, Derek was staring at his almost empty plate and yawning. Naptime had arrived.

"Go to the bathroom then head up to your room. I'll bring your bottle up and we can read a book."

Derek's eyes widened in surprise.

"Go, buddy. I'll be up in a minute. I just need to clean up the plates and get your bottle ready."

He finally shuffled out of the kitchen and down the hall to the small bathroom under the steps.

Five minutes later, I was walking into his room. Derek was on his bed, with his thumb in his mouth and his blanket and the blue superhero in his lap. He had the train book beside him.

I slid in next to him and pulled him close. He wiggled around a bit before finally finding a comfortable position at my side. I was able to pull him close with my left arm as his body curled tightly around my side. His blanket was obviously going to be a permanent fixture when he was little.

I had to coax his thumb out of his mouth before I could bring the bottle to his lips. He resisted the first two gentle tugs at his hand before he finally let the suction break. His apprehension about the bottle was evident when he wouldn't open for it, despite the nipple teasing at his lips. "It's okay," I offered. "Do you need to talk about it?"

Derek shook his head.

"Do you want Daddy to make the decision for you?"

Derek's body sagged into me as he sighed through his nose. He closed his eyes for a brief moment then nodded his agreement.

I could easily accommodate that request. "Buddy, open up for your bottle. You're sleepy and I know you want to read a book but we can't do that until you've had your milk."

Derek parted his lips and I let the nipple slide in. He clamped down on it quickly, his body clearly knowing what to do with it. In just a few seconds, he had a steady flow coming out of the nipple and I could feel tension leaving his shoulders. I would have loved to read while he had his bottle, but we weren't in the right position for me to be able to hold both a book and the bottle, so I settled on waiting for him to finish first.

Five minutes later, the sound of air being sucked through an empty nipple filled the room and I slowly pulled the nipple free. Derek's thumb went right back into his mouth and he handed me the train book he had found on the nightstand.

Not even four pages in, Derek had fallen asleep. I pulled the comforter over us and it didn't take long before I was pulled under by the sounds of his steady breathing.

CHAPTER 21

DEREK

As I woke up, I buried my face into the pillow and realized it didn't smell like my normal pillow. The memories of the late morning flooded back to me at the same time I noticed Colt's warm body holding me close.

I could get used to waking up like this.

The question on my mind was how I felt about everything we had done so far.

Going back through the morning, I thought about getting dressed in my play clothes, playing with trains on the floor while Daddy made lunch, eating lunch on a dump truck divided plate—*so cool*—and the sippy cup that matched. None of that stuff bothered me. I had felt safe and cared for and—*was it too soon to say it?*—loved.

We hadn't even had a conversation about if we were actually a couple and I was already feeling loved. My mind and heart were all over the place.

"What's wrong?" Daddy's sleepy voice asked from beside me. "You got tense."

I snuggled into Daddy's side and could feel his erection through his jeans. He didn't give me any indication he even felt how turned on he was, which I was thankful for, because I wasn't in the right frame of mind to do anything about it. My brain was foggy and I could feel myself being pulled down to that place I had been in before lunch, where all that mattered were my toys.

I found myself wondering how I would feel if a diaper was wrapped around me while I played.

"Just started thinking. Nothing's wrong, Daddy," I tried to make my voice sound like I meant it. In truth, nothing was wrong, everything felt right, and it was just confusing.

I could hear the skepticism in his voice when he asked, "Are you sure?"

I nodded. "Do I get to color now?"

"Let's go downstairs. I'll start a fire and you can color in the living room and watch some cartoons."

Daddy tossed a few of the throw pillows on the floor between the couch and coffee table so I didn't have to sit on the hardwood floor, and helped me get my coloring books and crayons out of my bag. I watched as he started a fire, but felt warm well before the fire was crackling.

Finally settled down, I opened my animal coloring book to the first page I hadn't finished yet. It was the picture I'd started with Daddy in mind. All the feelings I'd had while working on it the first time came rushing back to me. I wanted to color him the perfect picture to make him happy.

I had no idea how long I worked on my picture. I knew

three episodes of the cartoon had played on the TV and I'd finished a sippy cup of water. Measuring time in cartoons and sippy cups was *so* much better than looking at my phone constantly.

"Daddy?" I asked, looking up from my coloring book.

"I'm in the kitchen, buddy."

Standing up, I grabbed my blanket, cup, and the picture I had finally finished and made my way to him.

I stood at the island anxiously waiting for him to notice me. Daddy glanced up from the meatloaf he was making. "Do you need something?" He didn't sound annoyed, just curious about why I was standing in the kitchen instead of watching cartoons.

Holding out the picture to him I nodded. "I made you a picture."

Daddy smiled, the corners of his eyes crinkling slightly and his dimples appearing. "Oh, buddy, I love it. Thank you. Can I put it on the fridge?"

I nodded excitedly. "Uh huh!"

Daddy washed and dried his hands before he took the picture and hung it on the refrigerator.

I took a seat at the island and watched him making dinner. While I sat there, I felt how much more relaxed I was, but I wasn't feeling the need to have Daddy watching over me anymore. It took me a few minutes to understand I'd come out of the headspace I'd been in for most of the day.

Taking time to assess how I felt about being "big" but still wearing my little clothes, I decided I didn't much care. It would be incredibly uncomfortable if anyone aside from

Colt saw me like this, but I would have been uncomfortable if someone had seen me dressed like this no matter what headspace I was in.

I set my blanket down on the chair beside me and looked over at Colt. I hadn't said anything, and he was so engrossed in making dinner, he hadn't noticed I wasn't looking at him like he was Daddy anymore. He was gorgeous with his broad shoulders and trim waist. I didn't know how I'd gotten lucky enough to find a man who was kind and caring and seemed to like me just as much little as he did big. We hadn't had much time together with me being big and I wanted to rectify that as soon as possible.

It was far easier than it should have been to see a future with him. We had only known each other for two weeks and most of that time had been long distance. Yet, from the first time we started talking at the bar, I had been drawn to him. I wanted Colt and I wanted Daddy. Before I fell too hard for Daddy, though, I needed to make sure Colt and big Derek would be just as compatible.

No time like the present. "Can I help you with anything?" I asked.

Please don't ask me to actually cook anything.

Despite my mom's best efforts at teaching me to cook, I was a failure. I didn't want to embarrass myself in front of Colt so soon.

My voice must have held something different in it because the way he looked at me wasn't like he had looked at me when I was little. His eyes were darker and more intense. "Do you want to start peeling potatoes while I get this in the oven?"

"That, I can do!"

Colt quirked an eyebrow at my enthusiastic response.

I ducked my head and tried to fight off a bashful grin. "I'm uh, not known for my cooking prowess. I can sing, I can shake my hips well enough to get people screaming, I heft bales of hay and run heavy equipment on the ranch... but I am a bit of a disaster in the kitchen."

Colt laughed. "Good to know we need to stick to the basics, then. I guess it's a good thing I enjoy cooking."

I grabbed the bag of potatoes and began peeling them. It was refreshing how easily we seemed to fit together. Conversations were effortless. We discussed his work and mine and it felt like we had known each other for years before dinner was even made.

"When do you work next?" I asked as we sat down for dinner.

Colt looked uncharacteristically self-conscious. "I, uh, took the week off," he admitted before shoving a bite of meatloaf into his mouth.

"You took the week off?"

He nodded and the tips of his ears turned red. "You were so upset this morning when you called me. I called my deputy and told him I was taking the week off."

My eyes widened. "Wait, you took the week off, at the spur of the moment, for me?" My dad hadn't spoken to me since before I went on tour and this man I met two weeks earlier just took a week off from his job to be there for me. My emotions were swirling around like a tornado. I was grateful he'd realized I'd needed him, yet worried he thought I wasn't able, or mature enough, to handle what was going on myself. I'd been on the road alone since the beginning of the tour and had handled everything alone. My mom and brothers didn't even know half of the stupid shit that happened on a daily basis. I was feeling comfortable enough to open up to Colt, but was I relying too heavily on him? I didn't want to take advantage of him or his support. The thoughts left me not knowing if I should hug him or hit him.

"I have a lot of time saved up. The mayor has been on me for years to take some vacation. A week isn't that much."

Colt was a workaholic. I knew that because he was constantly getting calls or texts from work when we were talking. He just admitted he didn't take vacations, yet he took one because I needed him.

I decided to take it as a good thing and leaned over and kissed him softly on the lips. No tongue, no desire for more. It was simply a kiss of thanks I hoped conveyed how much his support meant to me.

Spending the rest of the evening hanging out at Colt's house was relaxing. After dinner, we'd each had a beer as I helped him clean up the kitchen. Our touches weren't as innocent as they were when I was little. Instead of gently placing a hand on my back like he did when I was little, he let it roam down and caress the curve of my ass. When we finally made it back to the living room, we didn't turn on cartoons, but found a show we both enjoyed and watched it while we talked about what my schedule looked like for the rest of the week.

Colt held me a little closer than any other boyfriend

had and he was always quick to jump up to grab drinks before I could even offer. I was beginning to understand that part of his personality was to be a caretaker. Around him, I was going to need to adjust to not being the decision maker. I had a feeling it wouldn't be difficult for me.

Before that night, I couldn't remember the last time I'd sat around and done nothing but watch TV. The last time I'd curled up with another guy was when my brother and I had an all night movie marathon before the tour started, that certainly didn't count, though.

Around eight, I decided I at least owed Harrison a text after walking out that morning and went to find my phone. I laughed when I caught a glimpse of myself in a mirror. The bright green didn't look bad with my skin tone, but the cut of both the shirt and pants was ridiculous for an adult. Though, seeing the words *Daddy's Boy*—even backwards in a mirror—sent a surge of happiness through me. I'd gladly wear this shirt any time. Big or little.

I swiped my phone off the dresser in the bedroom Colt had set up for me. Looking at the room through adult eyes, I could see all the little things he had done to make me feel welcome. The superhero bedding was nice, but it was the small matching nightlight on the dresser, and the way the lamp glowed softly in the dark room, that showed how much thought he had put into every piece. I pulled open the drawer that held the clothes and stared at them. They had all been washed, but it was easy to tell they were new. Colt—*Daddy*— had thought about what I would want, what size I wore, and what I needed. I didn't have to ask him to know this room hadn't looked like this before he met me. He'd done this hoping I would come to his house.

There was a man downstairs who wanted me for me. He didn't care if I was famous, he didn't care if I was little or big or if I called him Daddy or Colt. He just wanted me. Dinner had proven to me we had more in common than just our Daddy/boy relationship even though I was looking forward to exploring that particular interest further.

I powered on my phone. I didn't have any missed texts. Madeline must have threatened people with their lives if they bothered me. Thinking I probably owed Madeline a raise, I typed a quick message to Harrison.

Me: Hey, sorry I walked out today.

Harrison: OMG, Dare, are you okay? Madeline said you told her you were okay but not to bother you. It's been driving me nuts all day.

Me: I'm a lot better now. I slept most of the afternoon.

Harrison: Good! You've been a zombie the last few days.

Me: I know. I'm probably going to head to bed before long. I'm already getting tired.

Harrison: Are you sure you're up to meeting tomorrow? We can probably put off more stuff until later this week.

Me: I'll be good. Don't know if you're going to get a full day out of me, but I'll be there. We need to take more time off.

Harrison: Believe me, I know. We talked about it after Leslie left today, none of us want to extend the tour. We're already drained.

I sighed in relief. I was beyond grateful the rest of the band didn't want to extend the tour any more than I did.

Me: *See you tomorrow. Sorry again.*

Harrison: *Don't worry about it. See you tomorrow.*

I walked back downstairs with a smile on my face. Colt was sprawled out on the couch watching a football game and didn't notice me. I slipped quietly into the hall bathroom and pulled off my shorts and t-shirt. Looking down at my barely there briefs, I could see why they may not have been the most appropriate underwear for a little boy. Well, they may not have been appropriate for little Derek, but they were definitely appropriate for seducing my sexy man. My dick certainly thought so, too.

CHAPTER 22

COLT

I HAD GOTTEN SUCKED INTO THE TITANS' GAME ON TV and didn't realize Derek had come back downstairs until he was climbing on top of me. My eyes widened when I noticed his bare chest and legs as he straddled me. The sexy pair of lime green underwear barely containing his bulging erection was all I could focus on. Derek didn't seem to have any fat on him, which made me a little self-conscious about the few extra pounds that had appeared around my midsection in the last few years. No matter how many sit-ups I did, they seemed to stick around.

Derek's ass was rubbing me through my jeans which had become uncomfortably tight in a matter of seconds. I let out a moan as I thrust upward. The bite of the zipper through my underwear was just on the good side of painful. I wouldn't be able to do it too many times before getting sore, so I stopped myself with a low growl in my chest.

Derek leaned forward, bracing his weight on his arms

on either side of my body, and dipped his head for a kiss. Our lips brushed, tentatively exploring, but the kiss rapidly turned deeper. His lips parted and my tongue came out to find his. We battled for dominance for a moment before I gave in and let him lead.

Yes, I identified as a Dom, but I didn't have a need to be dominant all the time—it wasn't even something I desired. I liked to top, sure, but I was verse and was just as happy bottoming from time-to-time. Having Derek dominating the kiss and knowing how thick and well-proportioned his dick was to his body, I was itching to have him inside me. I planned on sitting back and letting him lead as much as he was comfortable. I was curious to see how far that would be.

Derek finally broke the kiss with a small nibble to my lower lip. Shimmying down my body, I felt his erection slide over mine, eliciting mutual groans. He glanced up at me, his eyes searching for any sign I might be against him going further. When he didn't see any sign of resistance, his hands came around to my belt. It was unfastened faster than I thought possible and he was already working the button of my jeans open.

He slid the zipper down carefully and began to ease my jeans off my hips. Once my dick was safely out of harm's way, the tortuously slow strip was over and he pulled them down my legs and off my feet, tossing them onto the recliner beside the couch.

"Fuck," he hissed, taking in the sight of my straining erection in my blue trunk boxers. "You're so fuckin' sexy," he breathed as he knelt between my spread legs and began unbuttoning my shirt from the bottom up. With each button he opened, he trailed a finger up my skin until he reached the next. The feather light touch of his fingers on my exposed skin sent chills up my spine. When he reached the last button, his hands came up and spread my shirt open, his fingers grazing my nipples as they moved the shirt to the side. I gasped and arched up into his touch and Derek's eyes sparkled.

Derek's fingers came back to my nipples and circled each bud in turn before using a finger to flick over the tips. My hips bucked off the couch and my dick jerked. Precum had already started beading at my slit. "Fuck, Dare," I hissed through my teeth.

A wicked grin spread over Derek's face. "You're so sensitive." He plucked roughly at my left nipple.

I gasped and felt precum soaking the front of my underwear. I was unable to form words and nodded frantically. I needed more, any way I could get it.

Derek bent and circled my right nipple with his tongue. Both buds were already hard points, and the feel of his warm, wet tongue followed immediately by a cool rush of air from his exhale had me screaming out with pleasure. I could feel my cock pushing against the fabric of my briefs, nearly in time with my racing heart.

"I bet I could make you cum just by playing with your nipples," Derek mused as I writhed and moaned beneath him. He'd found my hot button. I would do just about anything if my nipples were being teased, almost abused. "Fuck, Daddy, you're so hot. Your cock is leaking and I haven't even touched you." He freed my angry red shaft from my underwear, pushing them just below my balls, and stared down at it with appreciation. A sound close to a whimper escaped Derek as another bead of precum appeared at my tip.

Shit, who was this guy? Derek may have identified as a sub, but he had a dirty talking Dom locked not too far below the surface. Hearing him call me Daddy, though, reminded me he was still my boy and something in my mind latched onto that idea. No matter how assertive he was, he still needed his Daddy, needed *me* to be there for him when things became too much. It was the headiest feeling I could remember.

Derek brought me back to the present when he bit down on my nipple, sending jolts of electricity to my cock, then soothed the sting with a gentle lap of his tongue. I was dangerously close to cumming.

Derek looked up at me. "I want to make you cum like this and afterward, I want to fuck you."

And there was my submissive boy. Despite his dirty talk, he still wanted my permission to use my body. It wasn't in him to tell me what he was going to do to me. He was going to ask— make sure it was okay.

I had to find words, but my entire body was on overload. I could hardly get my brain to focus on his request much less form a response. Derek must have realized I had been close to flying because he slowed the torment on my nipples enough that I was able to focus on my thoughts. He slowly tormented me, occasionally plucking a hardened peak, waiting for my response. I had to find words and I hoped they made sense. "Yes, god, please. Yes." When I bottomed for someone, I liked it a little rough so that I felt it later. My nipples were definitely going to feel it the next day and I was loving it.

Derek bent over and nipped at my right nipple while caressing the left with the pad of his thumb. The warring sensations of rough and gentle had me right back to the brink of orgasm. I had never cum from nipple play alone, but the way my body was reacting, I knew that was likely to change.

He pulled back slightly and blew over the nipple he bit. "*Fuck,*" I gasped as my back arched off the couch. I grabbed onto either side of the couch cushion, trying to ground myself. I wasn't ready to cum, not yet. The relentless torture was too good. I wanted, *needed*, more.

"You like this," Derek murmured above me. "Mmm, nipple rings would be so hot."

Had he meant to say that out loud? I hadn't thought about nipple rings until just then, but the idea was delicious enough to have me wondering where the nearest piercing studio was. At least I was until he brought his lips down on my left nipple. Swirling the tip slowly with his tongue, he nipped, licked, and lavished my nipple like it was a dessert buffet.

I had become a mess of pleas and babbling when Derek reached across to my right nipple and pinched hard enough to make me scream out. Instead of pain, I felt intoxicating pleasure course through my body, straight to my dick, and I came.

"Fuck, Derek. Shit," I moaned as my dick pumped rope after rope of thick white cum between us. Derek continued to massage my nipples as my balls emptied. He didn't stop the delicious torment until my dick stopped pulsating.

He sat up and pulled a bottle of lube and a condom off the coffee table. I had no idea where they had come from, but I didn't have it in me to care. Derek pulled his briefs off his legs and tossed them on top of my discarded jeans. My underwear were fully removed and he was between my legs again. With the condom in one hand, he sheathed himself while he opened the bottle of lube with his other.

Pushing my legs up, he exposed my hole before he drizzled lube over my crack. Gathering some of the lube on his fingers, he circled my entrance a few times and tapped lightly at the puckered skin before sinking his thick index finger into me.

My spent cock twitched and jerked, trying to fill again as he worked his finger in and out, lightly grazing my prostate as he worked. Just as I began to regain my senses he added a second. His middle finger was able to easily peg my prostate with every thrust and he made sure to drag it along the bundle of nerves as he finger fucked me until I was hard and begging for him to fuck me.

"Derek!" I growled, gripping his arms with my hands. "I need you. Jesus Christ, fuck me."

"In a minute, Daddy. I need to make sure I don't hurt you." He was so sincere with his concern that I couldn't rush him. He scissored his fingers in my ass causing me to see stars behind my eyelids.

When he inserted a third finger, I almost came again. My ass clenched around his fingers and a strangled scream escaped my mouth. "Baby, I need your cock in my ass now or I'm going to cum."

Derek laughed. "Bossy."

"I'm a Dom," I growled unable to say more as his fingers slid out of my ass. Finally, *fucking finally*, Derek gripped his cock and used some of the extra lube to coat the condom. He adjusted himself on the couch so his left leg was near the back and his right was bracing himself on the floor then grasped the back of each of my thighs. Pushing my legs back, he slid into me slowly. My body knew it had just been wrung out from an intense orgasm, but it still wanted more.

"Shit, you feel good," Derek moaned as he bottomed out, his balls resting on my ass.

I grunted, his thick cock felt like it was splitting me in half. It had been a long time since I'd bottomed and my ass was reminding me of that. I was thankful Derek hadn't listened when I told him to fuck me when he had just worked the second finger inside me. He waited, his arms shaking, for my approval to move. After a few seconds, the pain turned to pleasure and I nodded.

His thrusts started out slow, giving me time to adjust to each of his strokes. The head of his cock massaged my prostate just enough that I could feel it with each push in. Within a few minutes, I was moaning again, my heavy cock slapping against my stomach as Derek continued to fuck me.

His pace picked up as his orgasm neared and he moved his thighs closer to my ass, causing my legs to move up slightly. With the new angle, Derek nailed my prostate relentlessly. I wrapped my hand around my cock, stroking myself in time with his thrusts. It wasn't going to take much to tip me over the edge at that point.

I knew Derek was close to cumming from the sounds he was making and the way his arms were beginning to shake while he loomed over me. "Cum with me," he grunted.

My body tightened as my orgasm ripped through me, my ass clenching around Derek's cock. I felt him tense then thrust into me with three more short, sharp bucks of his hips and he growled as he released into the condom. My own orgasm only produced a few small spurts of cum but it left me feeling like I had just run a marathon. Sleep was going to pull me under quickly and there wasn't anything I could do about it.

CHAPTER 23

DEREK

AFTER CATCHING MY BREATH, I PULLED OUT OF HIM, removed the condom, and tied it off. He was laying on the couch, chest heaving, with a far off look in his eyes. *Had I fucked his brains out?* I wondered if that was the same blissed out, unfocused look I had on my face after being thoroughly fucked. I had never tried anything like that with anyone before, but I felt comfortable enough to do it with Daddy. He told me what he wanted, even if it was just with a nod of his head. It felt like he was topping from the bottom and it was perfect. There was just enough freedom for me to explore, but I felt like he was still in control.

I was going to have to figure out why it was so easy to think of Colt as Daddy, even when I wasn't anywhere near little. It was as much a part of him as his job or his name. He was strong, assertive, and confident. Yet he was kind, caring, and loving. In my mind, the two couldn't be separated.

Making him cum by playing with his nipples, then fucking him until he had an almost dry orgasm definitely proved I was not in my little headspace. But calling him Daddy, even while fucking him, was natural. I lifted myself up from the couch and headed for the bathroom to find a trashcan and washcloths to clean us up. I washed myself first, tossing the used washcloth into a clothes hamper, and took a second one out to the living room to clean up my exhausted Daddy.

He was almost asleep when I got there, the Titans' game totally forgotten. A glance at the screen told me they were losing badly—and to Cleveland, at that—so it may have been better he didn't notice. The warm cloth made his stomach muscles ripple as I wiped him clean and he groaned softly.

"Do you want to go to bed?" I asked when I had our clothes and the washcloth picked up. It was close to nine and I was tired. I hadn't slept nearly enough in recent weeks and my body was begging for more rest.

Colt nodded slowly. "My room. I'm dead though, you may need to roll me there."

"Come on, Daddy. You gotta get up, you're too big to carry," I teased lightly as I took his hands and pulled him to his feet. He led the way to his bedroom where we both collapsed on the bed.

———

I HEARD my alarm ringing in the living room at 8:15 the next morning. I needed to be in Nashville by ten and I definitely needed a shower after last night. Colt did too, but he was still sleeping soundly beside me. Slipping out of his grasp, I made my way to my phone and shut the alarm off, then went upstairs to find my suitcase and grab a shower.

Colt knocked on the door as I was slipping a pair of bright purple cheeky briefs up my legs. "Do you need a ride to Nashville this morning?" he asked when I opened the door. His eyes widened when he saw my underwear. "Fuck, you own the sexiest underwear of anyone I've ever met," he growled.

I grinned. "Glad you like 'em." Growing up in Oklahoma and knowing I was gay had been hard on me. I never felt like I could tell anyone and homophobia ran deep in our community. My skimpy underwear, almost always in some ridiculously bright color, had been the way I expressed myself when I couldn't come out and say I was gay. In high school, I would wear boxers over whatever pair of underwear I chose on gym days, but bold undies had become part of my personal identity. Now as a successful adult, I spent more money on my underwear than I did on my clothing and I had no regrets about it.

"I can call a driver to get me to my meeting today," I said as I pulled an old t-shirt over my head.

"Don't be silly, I'll drive you. What do you want for breakfast? I have oatmeal." He laughed as my nose scrunched up at the suggestion. "What about eggs and bacon?"

"Yes, please!"

"Sounds good. Let me take a quick shower and I'll meet you in the kitchen."

While Colt took his shower, I checked my phone and took care of a few emails. When he joined me in the kitchen, we cooked breakfast together. More accurately, Colt made breakfast and I watched.

By 9:25 we were in the truck heading toward Nashville. I had a belly full of eggs and bacon and was ready to face the day. We talked throughout the ride into the city. I told Colt what I expected to happen at the meeting today. He shared his plans to work on some small projects around his house. It was comfortable, and I realized I would rather spend the day doing household chores with Colt than at my meeting. When we pulled up in front of the studio offices, I was reluctant to leave. Colt reached over and unbuckled my seatbelt.

"What time do you think you'll be done? I'll come pick you up."

"I don't have a clue. I'll text later." I leaned over and gave him a kiss as my phone rang. "Bye, Daddy have a good day," I said before slipping out of the front seat of his truck and answering my phone.

"Derek!" Madeline caught me before I made it three steps. I put one finger up.

"What's up?" I said into my phone.

Harrison was choking back a laugh at something. "Uh, just wondering when you'll be here."

"Now. See you in a few."

I ended the call and turned to my PA. "Hey, what can I do for you?"

"I haven't seen you looking so relaxed in weeks," she marveled.

I nodded. "I slept a lot yesterday."

"I'm sure your sexy 'Daddy' didn't have anything to do with you sleeping well."

I felt the color drain from my face. *Fuckity fuck fuck fuck, she knew something.* "Uh, what?" I stammered, voice nowhere near as calm as I wanted it to be.

She sighed. "Not the place to have this conversation, but, Dare, if you don't want people to know, you might want to try harder to hide that part of your relationship. I just heard you call him Daddy."

"Fuck," I groaned, pounding my head against the elevator wall. Thank fuck we were alone.

"You should probably have Colt sign an NDA."

"No." That was an easy answer.

"Dare, what if something goes south and he outs you as a kinky fuck?" She sounded like an exasperated mother. *Still did nothing for me.*

"I meant what I said, Maddie. No. I am *not* starting a relationship with someone by having them sign an NDA."

Madeline huffed at me but dropped the subject as the doors opened. "Later," she growled at me.

"Never," I responded, opening the door to the conference room and smiling at the group sitting around the table.

I started by apologizing to everyone for walking out the day before. I still felt guilty about it, despite what Harrison said. My apology was accepted easily and we moved on with the meeting.

"I think I can speak for us all," Gina spoke up, "when I say none of us are on board with extending the tour."

I nodded. "That's what Harrison said last night, as well. I don't want to extend it either. We still have over three months left and we're already tired."

Les looked less than happy and our management company rep looked like she had just swallowed a fly. Did other bands not say enough was enough sometimes?

"So, what's next on the list today?" I asked in an obnoxiously cheery voice.

Les cleared his throat and began talking about the possibility of recording a Christmas album when the tour wrapped up. I didn't hate that idea at all. I knew it would keep us in Tennessee for a little while and that, hopefully, meant more time with Daddy.

We ended up spending a ridiculously long six hours discussing Christmas songs. I had just gotten Jingle Bells out of my head from this Christmas barely six weeks earlier.

I sent Daddy a quick text as we finished up.

Me: *I think we're wrapping up soon. There's only so much Christmas we can discuss.*

Colt: *Okay, I'll head up that way.*

Twenty minutes later we were packing up.

"Wait, I want you to try to get the rights to a song for us," I said before the meeting came to a close.

The entire band, and Madeline, groaned, knowing exactly what was going to come out of my mouth. It started as a joke when I put on an old Christmas CD from a '90s boy band one night back in early December. They had written an original song for the album titled "At Home" and it had become something of a personal anthem for me throughout December. It was essentially about the singer being able to go home and be with the people he loved and didn't get to spend much time with. I played it before every show and sometimes after. I drove everyone nuts with it when I changed my ringtone to play the chorus. Though, knowing where I was going that night, the song felt far more personal and appropriate than ever before.

"Which song?" Les questioned, apprehension evident in his voice.

"NO!" everyone in the room yelled, throwing napkins and whatever else they could find at me while they laughed uproariously.

"At Home!" I managed to gasp out between my own laughs. "We have to get the rights to it."

A collective round of good natured groans went up around the room, but their heads were bobbing yes.

"At this point, it would be criminal to not add it. We only listened to it for the *entire* month of December," Harrison agreed.

"Now, I have a hot date tonight and he should be here soon."

Les promised he would see what he could do about getting the rights to "At Home." We packed up and said our goodbyes and Harrison and I headed for the elevator.

"Hot date with your 'Daddy?'" Harrison asked once we were in the elevator and heading toward the lobby. I had just taken a drink of water from the bottle I'd grabbed from the conference room and promptly spit it onto the elevator wall. *This damn elevator, I needed to start taking the stairs.*

"What?"

Harrison was doubled over laughing. "You swiped up before you said bye to your *Daddy* this morning. I heard that, so did the entire room. I need to meet Colt!" The elevator opened at the lobby to Madeline on the other side.

"Oh, I need to meet him too! He's got Derek making cartoon eyes at the mention of his name. And he hasn't signed an NDA yet," she reminded me.

"You've already met him," I retorted regaining my composure even if I was still embarrassed.

Madeline groaned. "Yes, I met far more of him than I ever wanted. I want to meet him with his clothes on."

"You met him in clothes while he was leaving the hotel and embarrassed yourself. You should probably just quit while you're behind."

"You're no fun."

I shrugged. "I know. And I already told you no to the NDA. How many more ways do you want me to say it?"

We exited the building and I shivered as the cold air hit my warm skin.

"Really? I just want you to say *yes*."

"I think you may be barking up the wrong tree," a deep voice said from behind us.

"Da-Colt!" I gasped as Madeline and Harrison started snickering behind me.

"You are a hot fucking mess, Derek Scott," Harrison laughed. "Hey, I'm Harrison. The OG best friend."

"Oh my god, Harrison, you're such a dork," I groaned

as I rubbed my forehead, praying for patience with my two insane friends.

Madeline laughed. "Jealous?"

Harrison nodded. "Yes, Dare is smitten with sexy Daddy here!"

He somehow managed to say that with a straight face.

"Bros before hoes doesn't work for Derek. Maybe, dude before Daddy?"

I was going to die of embarrassment. I was hoping the sidewalk would swallow me up and put an end to my misery.

Madeline held out her hand. "Madeline Stanley, personal assistant extraordinaire."

Daddy reached out and shook her hand. "Colt Westfield, Sheriff and Daddy. I've clearly stepped onto the crazy train, so I'm just going to ask... what were you guys talking about?"

I glared at Madeline who had no qualms about speaking up. "I think Derek should have you sign an NDA."

"No!" I almost yelled at the same time Colt said "Okay."

"No, I don't want you to." I crossed my arms and glowered at Madeline.

Colt looked baffled. "Why not? It's a paper that says I won't spill the beans on our relationship or anything we do. I wouldn't do that anyway."

"Exactly!" I threw my hands up in the air. "You wouldn't and I'm not going to have a contract to start our relationship!"

Harrison snorted. "Sounds like you may have one already."

My eyes shot up. "Harrison, we do *not* have a contract!"

Colt was laughing so hard he was turning red. "We'll discuss the *not* contract later."

Madeline crossed her arms. "You're his Daddy, make him see reason."

Colt shrugged. "I can only do so much. He's still his own man." Something seemed to dawn on Colt and he held up a finger. "Madeline, can I get your number? Last night, when Derek got to my place, we had to keep his phone on in case something important came up. It kept me on edge every time a notification came in while he was napping. If you had my number, we could turn his phone off and you could call me if something important came up."

Or playing, or eating my lunch, or having a bottle, I supplied in my head. The fact that he was able to make it sound *not* kinky or give away anything we had done the night before both calmed my nerves and surprised me.

"Yeah, no problem at all," Madeline said as she pulled her phone out of her pocket. She exchanged numbers with Colt before tucking her phone away. "Listen to your Daddy tonight," she told me with a grin as she turned away.

I knew she was trying to hint at Colt persuading me to let him sign the non-disclosure agreement. But my mind went straight to me being his boy and playing with my toys in the living room.

If I got any more embarrassed I was going to combust and Hometown would be out a lead singer.

CHAPTER 24

I WAS LAUGHING SO HARD I COULD HARDLY BREATHE. Derek's friends were fascinating. Harrison and Madeline had to make fabulous traveling companions. "Are they always like that?" I finally managed to get out.

"No. Something got into them today. Maybe a full night's sleep?"

I had to pull myself together before I could pull out of the parking spot. "Are they okay with you spending time with me?" Since both had referred to me as his Daddy and Harrison was talking about BDSM contracts, they had to know *something* about our relationship. It made it easy to introduce myself as Derek's Daddy to them.

Derek flopped his head back on the seat. "Yes, they know. I think you've just secured yourself as Daddy for as long as you decide to put up with me."

I laughed, but it wasn't hard to see myself sticking around Derek for the long haul, even with his crazy friends. "Are you okay with them knowing I'm Daddy to you?"

Derek shrugged. "I think Harrison just thinks it's a Daddy kink thing. Madeline may know more than I want her to know. Uh, the entire band knows I call you Daddy now, too. So there's that."

"They do?"

Interesting.

"I apparently accidentally answered the phone while telling you goodbye this morning," Derek mumbled, clearly embarrassed.

I shook my head in amusement, but decided it was time to change the subject. I also sensed Derek needed to know I wasn't laughing at him. I reached across the center console and took his hand from his lap. "Do you want to go out to dinner tonight? Or do you want to go back home?"

Home. That word felt right.

"Would you mind if we went home? I don't really feel like being *on* tonight."

I didn't need any crazy fanfare while eating dinner. There would be plenty of time for that in the future. Staying in worked well for me and we rode the rest of the way to my house in a companionable silence, holding hands the whole way.

We had only been home for five minutes when I heard the front door knob rattle.

"That would be my family," I warned Derek who had just come out of the bathroom.

"Oh, I get to meet Daddy's family." His eyes were sparkling with mischief.

Sleep had done wonders for the man's mood.

"Behave yourself."

I opened the door to my mom and sister holding a casserole dish, a covered bowl, and a bag.

"Hi?" I greeted them, still blocking the door.

"Why was your door locked?" Elise questioned.

"Because you guys need to learn boundaries. Why are you here?"

My mom sighed as she shoved past me and walked in, talking over her shoulder as she made her way to the kitchen. "Because I ran into Zander today and he said you took the week off unexpectedly. We figured you must be sick. Though you certainly don't *look* sick. But, my son hasn't taken a week off since he started at the Sheriff's office twelve years ago."

"I'm not sick, Ma," I said, following her into the kitchen.

"Then why did you take the week off?" Elise looked irritated that our mom had dragged her over to deliver food to someone who wasn't even sick. She dropped the bag on the counter with a thud next to where my mom had set the casserole dish and bowl.

Derek stepped up beside me and wrapped his arm around my waist. "It was my fault. I-"

The ear splitting squeal that came from my sister was enough to have all of us stepping back.

"D-Derek E-Edwards is, is in your house!"

Derek and I both nodded.

"Derek, this is my mom, Cheryl, and my little sister

Elise, she usually goes by Ellie though. Mom, Ellie, This is Derek Scott."

My mom wrapped Derek up in a hug and pulled back slightly, taking his face in her hands. "I don't care what you do for a living, but if you make my son take a week off work, then you're a keeper in my book!"

"Did you turn him gay?" Elise demanded.

"Elise!" Mom and I both growled.

Derek took it in stride. "No, he didn't turn me gay. I was gay well before I met him."

"Ellie, you don't get to go tell your friends. Our life isn't tabloid fodder. Got it?" I warned.

Ellie nodded like a bobble head doll. "Swear, my lips are sealed. So are you two, like, dating?"

Derek and I both looked at each other. We had never defined our relationship. I thought we were dating. I hadn't looked at another guy since I met him. But did he feel the same way? Judging by the way he was looking at me— expectant and hopeful mixed with a bit of apprehension—I thought it was a good guess he felt the same way I did.

Ellie cocked her head. "Or are you two just fuck buddies?"

"Elise Westfield!" My mom scolded.

"No, we are not *fuck buddies*. We're..." I trailed off

"Definitely not that," Derek agreed. "We're... together."

Together.

I smiled. "Yeah, we're together."

"Damn. You know, he's closer to my age than yours," Ellie mentioned.

"You're a minor and have the wrong anatomy for him," I snapped back.

"We're going to leave these with you and get out of here." My mom gestured to the food on the counter and ushered my sister out before she could say anything else to embarrass herself or me. Derek and I followed them back to the front door and I watched as they got into my mom's SUV.

When they were gone, I sagged against the locked door. "Sorry," I apologized. "They can be... nosey and a little intense."

Derek laughed. "They're awesome. They remind me of my mom and little brother."

We made our way upstairs and I helped Derek into a new pair of play clothes. This outfit was more form fitting. A thick diaper under the clothes while he sat at the coffee table playing with his blocks would have made the look perfect.

I plated up some of the food my mom had brought and took it to the living room. Derek didn't bat an eye at the sippy cup I gave him with dinner, but grinned when he discovered it was chocolate milk.

He wasn't quite little, but he definitely wasn't big, so I let his body language guide the evening. By ten, he had cleaned up his blocks and we were sitting on the couch watching an action movie on TV. Derek had his thumb in his mouth and his blanket in his fist but was taking every opportunity to wriggle around and his dick was noticeably hard through his shorts.

"Buddy, stop," I warned him as he squeezed his legs

together again. "You know you aren't supposed to be playing with yourself."

Derek whimpered and looked up at me with pleading eyes. "Daddy, I..." His words trailed off as he moved his butt back and forth on the couch, his breath catching as his cock rubbed against the material of his shorts.

"No, we're watching TV now and it's making it hard for Daddy to watch with a wiggle-worm next to me."

"Sorry, Daddy," Derek said, though he didn't sound all that sorry. His movements stopped for a few minutes, but by the next commercial break, he was back to rocking his hips and squeezing his legs together.

I reminded him to sit still again, and despite a little grumble of protest, he stopped... for the next two commercials.

"Buddy," I said in exasperation. "How many times am I going to have to warn you not to play with yourself? If you keep that up, you're going to end up over my knee. Naughty boys need to be reminded to follow the rules."

Derek's breath caught in his throat and his pupils dilated. I knew he'd liked the few times I'd playfully smacked his ass, but we'd never talked about punishments —fun or otherwise—when he was misbehaving. "That might be the only way I remember, Daddy."

His sexy voice and playful words went straight to my dick and I picked up the remote, turning the TV off.

"I see how it's going to be, then. My boy needs a reminder of how to listen to Daddy?"

Derek let out a long moan and thrust his hips into the

air again. "Yes, Daddy. I need..." He moved his hips in a slow circle. "That... yes... reminder..."

He was so far gone, I knew he wouldn't be able to hold himself back if he went over my lap in the living room, but I had something I thought might help in my room. "Go to my room and take off your shorts and undies and wait by the bed," I instructed him. "Do not touch yourself, buddy."

Derek groaned but climbed off the couch, his erection straining hard against his skimpy underwear and loose shorts. There was already a large wet patch of precum near the waistband. If I didn't get in there quickly, he was going to cum, spanking or not.

I gave him a thirty-second head start and then went to find him. He was standing next to the bed, naked from the waist down, his dick sticking out in front of him. "Good boy," I praised him for following directions. The two words caused his dick to jump and more precum appeared at the tip.

I crossed quickly to the dresser and pushed a few random items aside before I found what I was looking for. Taking it back over to my needy boy, I stopped in front of him. "You remember your safewords?"

"Yes, Daddy." He nodded frantically.

I held out my hand and showed him a narrow leather cock strap with snaps. The snaps would allow it to go on and off easily, even when he was aroused. Derek's eyes widened, clearly recognizing the item in my hand. "I'm going to put this on you, so you don't cum during your spanking."

Derek nodded again. "Yes... Daddy." His words were small and breathy.

I quickly wrapped the strap snuggly around his dick and balls, touching him as little as possible. With as turned on as he was, there was a chance he'd cum at the slightest touch. Thankfully, I was able to get the cock strap secured without him cumming.

Crossing the room, I took a seat in the wingback chair near the window. "Come here, buddy. Over Daddy's lap."

Derek crossed the room far slower than I had and paused as he reached me. His blue eyes were full of questions and a hint of apprehension.

"I'm not mad at you buddy. You have your safewords and you can use them if you need to."

He nodded slowly. "Okay. And you're not mad." He seemed to say the words more to convince himself than anything else.

"No, buddy, I'm not mad. But you weren't listening, and you kept trying to play with yourself didn't you?"

Derek nodded, this time with more certainty. "Yes, Daddy. I-I was naughty. I kept trying to play with my cock even though I'm not supposed to."

I fought to suppress a groan at his words. "Yes, now Daddy needs to help you remember not to do that. Over my lap, buddy."

My dick was so hard in my jeans it ached and I was at risk of cumming in my pants as he settled his body over my lap. His legs were on one side, his torso on the other, and his beautiful round ass up in the air. His breathing was ragged and his body tense with nerves, but his dick was still hard as a rock between my legs.

I ran my hand over the round globes of his ass, waiting for his body to relax slightly. In less than a minute, I felt the tension begin to leave his body and I quickly raised my hand and lowered it with a swift smack on his right cheek. I'd gone relatively light for the first smack, not wanting to push him too far too fast.

Derek's back arched off my lap and he moaned at the sensation. I brought my hand down harder on his left check. Derek's ass came up, practically chasing the next smack.

Smacks three and four were quicker and harder, his bottom beginning to turn a beautiful shade of pink from my hand. Derek groaned and tried to stay still for smacks five through eight, but by smack nine he was moaning loudly.

"Daddy, please!" he begged. I didn't know if he wanted more spankings or to cum, but I could tell by the way he arched into the last smack he was nowhere near asking me to stop.

"Have you learned your lesson?" I asked him as I landed smack ten at the sensitive patch of skin where his butt met his thigh.

"Yes! Yes, Daddy. Don't...yours." His ramblings made little sense, but I could make them out well enough.

I landed smack eleven hard on his crease and Derek cried out a beautiful moan of pleasure. As I raised my right hand for smack twelve, I brought my left hand that had been holding him gently against my lap, to the strap keeping his orgasm just out of reach.

As the last spank landed low on his butt, I flicked the snap open and said one word. "Cum."

Derek's body shook as his orgasm coursed through him. I held my right hand firmly on his reddened skin as his cock jerked hard between my legs. I could feel his cum soaking my pants. His thrusts providing just enough friction to my cock that he tipped me over the edge and my own orgasm tore through me, soaking my briefs and jeans.

As the last spasms of Derek's orgasm passed, he slumped down and lay across my lap like a ragdoll. "Buddy, I need you to get up," I told him after we both had a minute to recover. He nodded his head. "Bed...mm-hmm... up... soon."

I chuckled at his blissed-out brain fog. I gave him another minute to get his bearings back before having him stand up so I could help guide him to the bed. His movements were shaky and slightly uncoordinated, but I got him there safely and had him lay back.

"I'll be back in just a minute to get you cleaned up." He gave me a sleepy nod and I headed to the bathroom. Cum cooling inside my pants and between my legs was one of the most uncomfortable feelings I could remember. My boy needed me with him, so there was no time for a shower. I made do with a warm washcloth and some soap and felt quite a bit better in just a few seconds.

I took another washcloth out to the bedroom to clean Derek up. He was already asleep, his thumb pressed firmly in his mouth. He'd been so tired he hadn't even realized his blanket was still in the living room. I cleaned him up gently, trying not to wake him, then went to grab his blanket.

After making sure the doors were locked, I went back to the bedroom and slipped into bed next to him. I covered his chest with his blanket before pulling him close to my body and falling asleep almost as quickly as he had.

CHAPTER 25

DEREK

AFTER FOUR PERFECT NIGHTS WITH DADDY AT HIS house, Friday dawned gray and gloomy and as I kissed Colt goodbye in the truck in front of the label's headquarters, snow began to fall. It wasn't the fluffy white snow that coated everything in a shimmering blanket either. It was the cold, wet, half rain, half snow that froze you to the bone on contact. I was still shivering from the walk to the building when our manager John walked into the conference room where the band had gathered as he finished up a phone call.

He was a portly man with thinning hair, glasses, and a double chin so large you couldn't see his neck. John had been with us from the beginning, though none of us could seem to remember *why* or *how* we had gotten placed with him. The longer he spent with us, the less we liked him. Looking back, I should have pushed for someone else the first time he made a snide remark about a gay man. At the time, Hometown had been so new I was nervous to speak up.

"It's wrong," he said, as he shook his head. There was a brief pause and he continued. "No, no one needs to have that shit shoved in their faces. What they do in their own time is their own business but keep it out of the media."

He was turning red as he spoke, and we glanced around trying to figure out what was going on. Madeline pulled her phone out of her pocket and started tapping furiously on the screen.

"The fuck?" Harrison mouthed to me. I didn't care for John all that much, but this was unprofessional, even from him. Whatever this conversation was about should have been concluded before he walked into the conference room with us.

"There's a code of conduct that all those in the public eye should abide by," he continued, seemingly unaware of the group of us sitting at the table. "That includes men fucking other men."

My blood ran cold and the briefest glance at Harrison showed he had paled noticeably.

"Queers have no right shoving it in everyone's faces," John growled.

My mouth dropped open in shock and Gina reached over and squeezed my arm. Everyone in the room knew I was gay. The audacity he had to bring his homophobia into our conference room was beyond unnerving.

"I will *not* tolerate our clients behaving in such a disgraceful manner."

It was an eye-opening moment for me. I'd suspected

John may have some fairly ignorant views on homosexuality, but this took it to a whole new level. John wasn't just ignorant, he was clearly homophobic. To top it off, he *owned* the management company.

Harrison looked more uncomfortable by the second. His hands were balled in front of him and I was pretty sure he was holding back tears. I wished I could pull him into a hug like I knew would help calm him, but I also didn't want to draw more attention to him. We'd all walked on eggshells around Harrison's relationship status. It was clear to everyone on tour he had something going on with one of the backup musicians—my gut said it was our fiddle player, Neil.

Madeline tapped me on the shoulder and moved her phone toward me when I looked at her. She had a TMZ article on the screen of two men holding hands under a table in a restaurant. The photo had clearly been taken with a long-lens camera and caught the Hollywood hunk and, a guy who I assumed was his boyfriend, in a private moment when they thought they were being stealthy.

Fucking paparazzi.

Gina leaned as far over the table as she could to try to see what was on Madeline's phone. Her face contorted in confusion and anger as she shot death glares John's way. He was oblivious to us as he continued to pace and seethe about the "mess" he was going to have to "clean up."

My heart went out to the guy who John's company represented. He was going to have a hell of a time navigating the situation he was in when the owner of his management team was clearly showing his true colors in our conference room.

I tilted my head toward the door and pushed back from the conference room table. Thankfully, Gina, Madeline, and Harrison followed silently. We had gathered to discuss some of the fallout from the disastrous show in Lexington. I knew it was coming and we were trying to come up with a solution to the negative publicity. That had rapidly taken a backseat to the current... issue. A two-hundred-fifty pound issue named John Sampson who was near coronary status while seething about having to deal with a gay client. I almost wanted to call the poor guy and warn him about the temper tantrum John was having in the middle of the conference room.

I scrubbed at the back of my neck uncomfortably. "Uh, what do we do?"

"You guys take him out, Madeline and I can find a place to hide the body," Gina said in a frighteningly serious tone.

At least it got Harrison to crack a smile. "Too many witnesses."

"Shit. It sounded good to me."

I rolled my eyes. "We aren't the mob. We need a non-violent solution here."

Gina sighed dramatically. "He's getting a significant amount of money for managing Hometown. He's an asshole."

Harrison scoffed. "He's been an asshole since day one. Leslie and the rest of the label didn't give us much of a choice on who we used. They just kind of threw him at us."

"And he's been a dick since I met him," Gina piped in. "He's in there blowing a gasket because a guy in Hollywood—one of the most eccentric cities in the country—is holding hands with another man. What would he say if pictures of you ever got out?"

I sighed, that was a damn good question. I didn't want to believe I had the answer already because it was a hard pill to swallow, but I saw how he was reacting to a picture of two men holding hands. The thought of a picture turning up of Colt and me together while John represented us soured my stomach. My fear that the first picture to surface would be of Harrison and Neil was even greater than my fear the picture would be of Colt and me.

I was at the point in my life I had accepted my sexuality and I was out to my family and friends. Harrison hadn't even confirmed to me he was dating Neil, despite the fact that I was sure he was.

Madeline was uncharacteristically quiet through the entire discussion. I looked over at her to find her deep in thought. "Listen, I can only speak as an outsider, you guys are the ones paying this homophobic prick to manage you, but I see a few things going on here. First, he's acted like a child since day one. Every time he doesn't get his way, he throws a fit until someone caves. Like your name," She shot me a look.

Yeah, I hadn't liked putting Derek Scott away to become Derek Edwards. At the time I thought I understood why we were doing it, but we had just delayed the inevitable at that point. Beyond that, separating my real self from my stage name put a lot of shame on me for my sexuality and for the first time in years, I'd had a hard time accepting the fact I was gay.

"He's also sneaky about doing things behind your backs. How many times have you all caught him in a lie?"

Gina growled. I didn't even have to ask what she was thinking about because I knew it was the time we found out he'd been the one to leak photos of her kissing one of the crew members backstage. We still hadn't figured out *why* he'd done it, but I suspected it was to get our name into the spotlight since we had just begun the tour. It was barely a blip on most people's radar, but it had bothered Gina deeply.

Madeline sighed. "Derek, it's just a matter of time before something comes up about your relationship with Colt. If you keep seeing him, there are going to be pictures, no matter how careful you are. A fan can be anywhere, and a picture of a country music singer kissing or holding hands with another man is going to bring in a pretty penny. Do you all really want him to be representing you when that happens?"

I was glad she hadn't brought Harrison's relationship up. I wasn't going to let someone out him until he was ready. He'd been my best friend since we started school and he would've done the same thing for me if our positions were reversed.

The three of us shook our heads in unison. There was no way I'd be comfortable having to face country music fans or the media with John at my side when—not if—my relationship with Colt was discovered.

Shit we were in trouble.

"I didn't think so. So that leaves you needing to terminate your contract with him."

"How do we even go about doing that?" Harrison wondered, staring at the closed conference room door.

"There has to be conflict of interest somewhere," Gina stated.

I nodded. "And there has to be enough evidence of the stupid shit he's done before this to get the contract voided. Leaking those pictures to the press of you alone should be enough to get him for a breach of the non-disclosure agreement he signed." *Why hadn't we terminated the contract after that incident?* The only answer I could come up with was that we had been too green and stupid. Well, that was going to end immediately.

"You get the band's attorney involved," Madeline spoke up. "I can text her now."

"Do it," Harrison and I said at the same time.

"Now we tell John to get the fuck out. I don't even want to look at his ruddy face anymore. That man makes me sick," Gina grumbled.

We had to go back inside the conference room, but when I put my hand on the doorknob, I purposely kept Harrison behind me. Even if he was bigger than me, I had the same draw to protect him as I did to protect my younger brother. John was still ranting about his Hollywood client as the door shut. The audible *click* of the door must have alerted him to our presence—finally—and he looked up to see us standing just inside the room.

"Mark, I've gotta go," John said into the phone. "The band just walked in. Only fifteen minutes late... yeah, bye."

Gina's nostrils flared. "Late?" she asked, her tiny fists balling at her side.

"You were supposed to be here," he looked at his watch, "fifteen minutes ago."

"You're an idiot," Gina sputtered.

I shook my head in disbelief. "We were here. You walked right by us while you were throwing your little hissy fit. We were *all* sitting at that table." I pointed to the table in front of us. Yes, it was a large table that could have sat twenty businessmen. Yes, we had been seated at the far end, but that still didn't explain how he'd missed us.

John looked shocked, and I guessed he was hoping we had been lying. "Impossible."

Gina tapped her chin. "Do the words, 'Queers have no right shoving it in everyone's faces,' ring any bells to you? You realize the lead singer of this band, the one that helps pay your bills, is gay, right?"

I nodded. "The problem is, I haven't shoved my sexuality in your face enough. Had I been me around you, I'm pretty sure I would've figured out you're a bigot a long time ago, and we wouldn't be standing here over a year after meeting you, telling you you're fired."

John's face flared even redder than it had been before. "You can't do that, we have a contract."

Madeline shrugged her shoulders and smiled.

"According to Natalie, you voided that contract when you leaked the picture of Gina four months ago."

"That was for your own good!" he roared, spit flying out of his mouth as his hands flailed wildly about.

It was getting harder to keep my cool, but the last thing I needed was to end up on the front page of the gossip sites for decking the idiot in front of us. "We're done. We put up with your shit too long."

John grabbed his briefcase and stormed passed us. "Fucking entitled queers. How did I get stuck with the gay ones?" he was clearly muttering as he passed us. He looked over at me and snarled then shot an icy glare at Harrison. "It's only a matter of time before one of you fucks up and your love lives are all over national news."

"That had better not have been a threat," Gina snapped, bouncing forward almost three full steps before Harrison and I managed to catch her arms.

"Let him go," Madeline whispered. "I recorded it." She smirked devilishly as John turned white and stormed out of the room. The door slammed with such force a picture fell off the wall causing all four of us to jump.

"I think I need to go home," Harrison said, and I agreed completely. Harrison had always found inner peace being on a working ranch. After witnessing the disaster that had just stormed out of the room, I knew he was going to need space from all of this to process his feelings. He needed to figure out if his relationship with Neil was worth the potential public backlash if it was discovered.

It was going to be our job, as a band, to find a way to give him the chance.

"How catastrophic do you think it would be to take next week off?" I asked.

Gina shrugged. "Fans will be pissed, Les and the others will probably be worse. But it needs to happen." She shot Harrison a sympathetic look.

Harrison looked shell shocked and I knew how it felt because I'd been there on Monday.

"I'll get us a flight home," I told Harrison. I glanced at Madeline who was already tapping away on her phone.

"I'll let you know when the flight is booked," Madeline told Harrison.

"I'm going to get out of here," he said. "Will you all be able to handle the other shit?"

Gina waved him off. "Go on. Get out of here."

We agreed to take a ten-minute break before we dragged Les and the others who needed to know what was happening into the room to tell them the changes in our plans. I took the time to let my boyfriend—I loved being able to call him that—know about the change.

I smiled when I reached our text conversation. I had changed his contact the night before from Colt to Daddy. I hadn't thought of him as Colt in days. He didn't seem to mind me consistently calling him Daddy, it felt natural no matter what headspace I was in at the time.

Me: *Shit exploded. Will be done soonish. Don't know exactly when.*

Daddy: *On my way. What's up? Do you need anything?*

Me: *A new manager. Long story.*

Unfortunately, telling the management teams we were

taking a week off went about as well as we'd expected. There was a lot of yelling, a lot of cussing, and when they found out we were terminating our contract with John there was even more yelling.

Their protests fell on deaf ears. They had finally pushed us too far.

CHAPTER 26

COLT

DEREK WAS IN A FAR BETTER MOOD AS HE LEFT THE studio than I had expected him to be after receiving his texts. He climbed into the truck and leaned over to kiss me. "It's been a hell of a day. I can't even begin to figure out where to start," he sighed. "I'm heading to Oklahoma with Harrison in the morning. He's had a rough day and I don't want him traveling alone."

If Derek was worried enough about Harrison to feel he needed to go back to Oklahoma with him, I was going to support him. "Is Harrison okay?"

"Honestly, Daddy, I don't know. I think he's dating Neil, the fiddle player. I haven't pushed because no one wants to be forced out of the closet. I know I didn't. Well, our asshole manager came damn close to outing him today."

"Fucker," I grumbled under my breath.

Derek exhaled. "I'm frustrated we didn't pay more attention to the warning signs that have been there all along. I'm pissed the guy that has been getting a cut of our profits hasn't just been ignorant, he's homophobic."

My boy was composed and rational, a totally different guy than the one who had called me crying on Monday morning. Throughout the week, I had watched him blossom into the guy I had met at the bar, and even beyond that. He was witty and had great stories to tell about his friends. Having had the ability to regress when he needed to was helping him deal with the other shit in his life with a smile on his face.

"Okay, well, we'll get you home and packed up tonight so you're ready to go first thing in the morning. What time do you need to be at the airport?"

"Seven," he groaned.

As we drove home, Derek filled me in on the rest of the meeting with his band and the management team. I continued to be impressed by how much Derek had to handle on behalf of the band, and I started to wonder if maybe a different team would have done a better job of taking some of the pressure off him. I was glad they had decided to find someone new to manage them.

When we got home, we reheated some of the leftovers from the food my mom had brought over and by the time we finished eating, Derek was ready to relax for the evening. All he wanted to do was sit on the couch and watch cartoons, at least until I grabbed my tablet and opened up a clothing site geared toward littles.

"What's that?" he asked, moving his thumb to the side just enough so he could be understood.

"It's the site I got your pajamas from, but they have other stuff too."

Derek looked curiously at the front page. "Yeah? Like what?"

I tapped the icon I knew would take us to the adult training pants.

Derek's eyes went wide when the numerous options appeared on the screen. "You were serious! They actually make those in my size!"

I nodded. "They do. Would you like to help me pick them out? Or would you like me to surprise you."

"Help," Derek stated without hesitation.

He curled even closer to me and I put the tablet between us. We spent the better part of an hour picking out training pants for him. He seemed to grow more excited as we looked at the options. Once we found three separate pairs with trains on them, Derek was convinced. Of course, that was just the tip of the iceberg. He found another pair with a spaceship that reminded him of his favorite cartoon, a pair with a dump truck, and a few others. I didn't really know that he *needed* as many pairs as we ordered, but he couldn't seem to narrow his choices down past what we had in the cart.

I waited for the confirmation email to be sent before I made him a bottle of milk for bed. He was yawning and was going to have an early morning the next day.

After he drifted off with his thumb in his mouth and his blanket wrapped around his upper body, I watched him sleep for a few minutes. I was going to miss my boy when he was gone.

CHAPTER 27

DEREK

The flight from Nashville to Oklahoma City took two hours and from there it was almost another hour in the car to get to our hometown. Harrison and I fed off each other's unease. He was dealing with whatever personal stuff he was going through and I hadn't wanted to leave Daddy. The goodbye at the airport drop-off had left me emotional all the way to the gate.

Harrison reached over and grabbed my hand while we were on our way to our childhood homes. "You know, you didn't have to leave Colt. You could have stayed in Tennessee with him for the next week."

I shook my head. "You needed a friend more. I'm here for you. Daddy agreed with me anyway," I told him with a wink. Calling Colt 'Daddy' in front of Harrison was still uncomfortable, but the bark of surprised laughter Harrison let out was worth the mild discomfort.

We reached his family's ranch first and we both slid out of the back seat to greet his family with hugs. I finally pulled Harrison in for a tight embrace. "Call me if you need *anything* this week."

He nodded slowly. "Thanks, Dare. Talk soon."

Five minutes later, I was climbing out of the SUV in front of my childhood home. The ranch had grown considerably since my older brother had taken over daily operations from our dad. He had a business degree and was putting it to good use. He had already expanded the 500-acre ranch to 1500 acres in the span of only a few years.

My mom came flying out the front door and engulfed me in a hug. "You're earlier than I expected!"

"The flight was actually on time and Madeline had a car waiting for us." I yawned while I unloaded my bag and backpack from the trunk.

My mom rolled her eyes. "Go to bed before you fall asleep standing in the driveway."

I wasn't going to argue and headed to my room with my bags. I stripped down to my black briefs with rainbow hearts on them. They weren't the sexiest pair I owned, but they made my ass look amazing. I ran my hands over my butt and wondered what I would look like in the training pants we had ordered the night before.

I had gotten so used to Daddy getting me ready for bed and putting me into pajamas that sleeping in briefs felt... weird. I realized I had forgotten to let Daddy know we'd landed and I grabbed my phone to send a quick text.

Me: *I should have brought some of my PJs with me.*

Daddy: *We will remember that next time. I take it you made it safely?*

Me: *Yep. Going to take a nap now. Miss your snuggles.*

Daddy: *Sleep well, buddy. I miss you, too.*

I didn't wake up until I smelled lunch and heard the clatter of dishes. I forced myself to roll out of bed and begin functioning because my stomach was growling. Jeans felt like too much of a hassle for home, so I slipped on a pair of well worn sweatpants and left my room.

Not only did not wearing pajamas feel weird, but leaving my blanket in my room felt like I had left an appendage behind.

My mom, dad, both of my brothers, and my younger brother's best friend, Declan, were in the kitchen loading plates with food when I finally joined them.

"Good afternoon!" Mom greeted me with a smile as she handed me a plate which I immediately started filling with lunch items.

I sunk into the chair between my brothers once my plate was filled. Jasper was twenty-five and liked to tease me about being older. Now that we were both over twenty-one, it was a lot more fun to rub in that he was older than me and it always made him grumble. "How have things been, old man?" I asked him. There was so much food on my plate I couldn't decide where to begin.

He shrugged his shoulders. "Eh, same old same old." He studied my exposed arms for a few seconds. "Jesus Dare, did you move into a gym? Your biceps are twice the size of mine!" he said as he squeezed my upper arm.

I flexed a muscle proudly. "I learned the value of peace and quiet... unfortunately, the only place I get it is in the gym."

I turned to my younger brother and elbowed him playfully in the ribs. "What about you? How have you been?"

Ty shrugged. "Fine, nothing going on other than school and work." Ty hated ranch work, but he loved animals. Even as a kid he didn't seem to care much about the operation our dad ran. Instead, he had always followed the vets around and spent every spare second he could with the animals. He was smart, loved a challenge, and it was obvious small-town life wasn't for him. Ty wasn't simply going to go to college, he was going to run. I highly doubted he would look back, either.

Ty's best friend, Declan, was sitting at the table like he was part of our family. It wasn't far from the truth. His parents owned a house a few miles away and he and Ty had been best friends since kindergarten. The two were practically inseparable and due to a bad family situation, Dec had been at our house for most of the school year.

My mom let it slip Declan had enlisted in the Navy and would be leaving right after they graduated in June. I worried about how Ty would handle that move. I couldn't even remember the last vacation we had taken that Declan wasn't with us. It would be a shock to both of them when Declan went to Chicago and Ty went to Colorado for college.

My dad didn't even acknowledge my existence and, while expected, it still hurt.

"What are your plans for this week?" My mom asked as we finished our meals.

A week ago, the answer would have been an emphatic, "Sleep!" but at that point, I didn't know exactly what I was going to do. Without Daddy around and without a tour schedule, I honestly felt a little lost.

"I should probably try to reconnect with some friends while I'm here. It's not like I'm home much. Maybe I'll see if some people want to go out tonight."

"The bowling alley got remodeled," my mom supplied.

And that *is how you know you grew up in a small town.*

We chatted and caught up over the rest of lunch and as the meal ended, I'd fallen back into the rhythm of home.

"I'll help you clean up the kitchen," I told my mom as my dad grumbled about work to be done and Jasper followed close behind.

Ty and Declan headed for Ty's room to work on homework.

"Is it just me or is there something between those two?" I asked my mom when we were alone.

"Ty and Dec?" she questioned, looking at the steps they had run up.

"Yes, they were practically eye-fucking each other across the table."

Mom shrugged. "Ty has a girlfriend... for now." She seemed as skeptical about Ty's relationship as I did.

By the time the kitchen was cleaned up, my phone had been buzzing in my pocket for fifteen minutes. News travels fast in a small town and Harrison and I returning home was big news. There was a group of friends meeting at, *of course*, the bowling alley that evening.

BEING able to hang out with friends who knew Harrison and me before we were famous made it far too easy to lose track of time. Beer flowed freely, but I was careful about how much I drank. The last thing I needed was for a picture to show up in the tabloids of me shitfaced.

Or to have me spill the beans about Daddy, a little voice reminded me.

Harrison only had a few drinks as well, but he seemed far more relaxed than he had been when we arrived in Oklahoma earlier that morning. We didn't have a lot of time to talk privately, but his easy smiles and deep laughs spoke volumes about his mood. If I knew Harrison, he'd spent the day working on his parents' property, likely scrubbing animal stalls. He was the only person I knew who found that particular job relaxing. Mucking stalls was Harrison's version of age play. It was the way he let his mind wander and relax.

Ty and Declan had caught a ride with me and were bowling with their friends. Despite Ty's girlfriend being at the bowling alley, Ty was paying far more attention to Declan than he was to her. Even while she was sitting on his lap with his arms wrapped around her, Ty's full attention was on Dec. The two had always been affectionate with each other—hugs, bumping their shoulders or knees together, hell Ty would still drag Declan around by the hand like he had when they were kids—but that night, I noticed the touches seemed a little more deliberate... meaningful even. And they weren't one-sided. Declan was just as guilty as my brother.

Interesting.

Between talking with friends and watching Ty and

Dec, time slipped by quickly. I had intended to head home before ten to talk to Daddy before it got too late, but I had missed that by over half an hour.

Making my excuses, I caught Ty's attention to let him know I was leaving. He and Declan had a quick conversation and Ty jogged up to me alone.

"Is Dec not coming?"

Ty shook his head. "Nah, he's going to go to Mark's house to play some video game that just came out. I don't like multi-person shooters. You're stuck with me."

We walked out into the cool night and headed to the truck in the parking lot. I took a deep cleansing breath. I could understand why Harrison needed to come back home, there was something oddly comforting about the air here, the feelings of familiarity even if the bowling alley had been remodeled.

"Your girlfriend seems nice," I said tentatively as we headed home. I was curious to see what Ty would say about her.

Ty grinned. "She's nice. She's spontaneous and easy to talk to."

That was an interesting, almost clinical, way to describe her. Did he not even realize how strange that sounded? *Nice* and *spontaneous* could describe a large portion of the population. If someone asked me to describe Colt I'd have more adjectives than I'd know what to do with—sexy, gorgeous, dominating, intelligent, kind, thoughtful... *Daddy.*

Ty changed the subject before I could continue my questioning. "How's the tour been?"

I laughed. "Stressful. Since Christmas, especially, it's been difficult. It's still new, so don't go blabbing this, but I met someone."

The corners of Ty's mouth went up. "Oh, the guy you were being cagey about? Mr. 'He lives in Tennessee'?"

I'd forgotten all about that uncomfortable phone call until just then. "Yes, that one."

Ty seemed giddy with excitement. "Tell me about him. How'd you meet?"

I pulled over and parked the truck so I could talk to him without the fear of one of our parents hearing me. For the next twenty minutes, we sat on the side of the driveway leading to the main house and talked about Colt. By the time I pulled the truck into drive, Ty knew almost everything about him—though I may have left out a few important details.

"Sex is pretty fucking amazing, too," I said with a waggle of my eyebrows.

"Dude, if he's as sexy in bed as you have described him fully clothed, I can't even imagine," Ty said with a laugh.

I parked my truck near the garage and we stepped out into the night. The crickets were almost deafening and a full moon illuminated the clear night sky.

"When can I meet him?" Ty asked as we walked toward the front door.

"I don't know, hopefully soon."

"Why didn't he come with you?"

"He would have if I had asked, but I didn't want to guilt him into coming. Besides, I haven't told Mom yet, Dad hasn't spoken to me since I came out, and Jasper was really weird about it when he found out. Colt took last week off work to spend time with me so I don't think he could take another."

"Bummer."

I shrugged. "You're the first one here who knows. Like I said, it's new, but I like him a lot. Now, I need to try to catch him before he goes to bed."

"Tell him I want to meet him," Ty said as he walked to his room down the hall.

I walked into my room long enough to throw on some sweats and text Daddy.

Me*: You awake?*

Daddy*: Yup. Just started getting ready for bed.*

I grabbed my blanket and headed down to the enclosed porch. I flicked the heater on and snuggled into the couch as I made the call.

"Hey, buddy," Daddy answered on the first ring.

I smiled as my body instinctively relaxed at the sound of his voice. "Hey, Daddy. I miss you."

CHAPTER 28

COLT

Until earlier in the week, I'd never been called Daddy outside of a scene. At first, it confused me slightly. I didn't know if he was in his little headspace or not. Once I figured out that to him, Daddy was synonymous with Colt, it became easier. After a few days of hearing him call me Daddy it was becoming second nature.

"Did you have fun with your friends tonight?"

Derek laughed. "Yes, Daddy. I had a lot of fun with my friends." There was a playful tone to his voice and I realized how the question had sounded.

"You know what I meant." I was pretty sure the eye roll was evident in my voice.

"Yeah, it was nice. I haven't seen some of those guys in a few years. I got to spend some time with Ty since he and Declan tagged along. What did you do today?"

Did I tell him my mom had spent the afternoon at my house grilling me about our relationship? She had commandeered my kitchen, made cookies, and quizzed me for over an hour. By the time she was satisfied with the information I'd given her, I had a sinfully large container of fresh baked cookies on the counter and was thankful I hadn't told her about the more interesting parts of our relationship.

I decided against it. "It was good. Did a lot of laundry. *Someone* seems to make a lot of it."

Derek's laugh echoed through the phone. "*Someone* likes dressing me up."

"Touché." He was simply too cute and he liked the outfits I bought him. He didn't need to know I had my tablet propped up on my lap as I scrolled through a website with more clothes I thought he might like.

"I told Ty about you tonight," he admitted.

"How'd that go?"

Derek chuckled. "It went well. Truthfully, I think there is something going on between him and Declan. They keep giving each other bedroom eyes. It's weird because Ty has a girlfriend. But if you'd have seen them together, it's... strange."

"You have to let him figure his own stuff out. He may be gay, he may be bi, he may be curious, or he may be completely straight. I've never met him, so I can't tell you with any degree of certainty. Just give him time."

"Honestly, I am fairly certain Ty is at least bi. What worries me is he only seems to have eyes for Declan. We've all fallen for the straight guy and I don't want Ty to end up hurt."

Derek went silent for a moment before sighing, "Personally, I hope Ty stays in the closet until he leaves. I don't want him to deal with the same shit I've dealt with."

"What happened with your dad?" I finally asked. Derek had told me they weren't on speaking terms. I knew it bothered him, but I never pried into that part of his life and it was always a giant question mark for me. Derek seemed chatty and I got the feeling it was eating at him now that he was home.

"Ugh, it's a fucked up situation. I hadn't meant to come out when I did. I was so stressed out about leaving, about the tour, and about life. My world had been Oklahoma until we signed the record deal. Then boom, we were on the radio, we'd toured as an opening act, we were setting up a headlining tour. In the back of my mind, my sexuality kept eating at me. It's hard enough to have cameras pointed at you for the first time. But knowing I was hiding this huge part of me from the world was scary. And homophobia in the country music scene runs rampant."

I could understand all of those concerns. I lived in Tennessee. I'd heard it all. Coming out as a teenager was stressful and making a career in law enforcement as an out gay man had been challenging. I'd had it easier than many, but I still had slurs thrown at me from time to time. The ones that hurt the worst were from officers from other jurisdictions. For some people, my career and achievements would always be overshadowed by who I was attracted to. I had thick skin, but that hadn't stopped me from collapsing on my parents' couch a time or two after a rough day because it hurt like hell to hear someone I knew call me a queer, or a fag, or a host of other slurs.

I couldn't imagine what it would be like to have the world know my name and worry about millions of people judging me for who I was attracted to. It was a heavy burden to carry around.

"It just came out one night. I told my mom before I even realized what I'd said. When my dad found out, he lectured me about how I would go to hell. Hearing him tell me he was disappointed in me hurt just as much as the fact he can't even look at me anymore. I haven't had a call or text from him since I left for this tour." The hurt was evident in Derek's voice as he whispered the last few words.

"I'm so sorry, buddy."

"I know, Daddy. It is what it is. I can't change him." He said it with such finality and resignation in his voice I wished I could wrap him up in my arms and hold him. "I don't want Ty to go through what I've gone through. My dad isn't heartless, he's just set in his ways. I haven't had to live here since I came out and it still hurts to see that look on his face when he sees me. I can't imagine having to see it every single day for the next six months."

I hated being so far away from him. I needed to change the subject before I was on a plane to Oklahoma to be with my boy. "Do you have any other plans for the week?"

"Avoid the city as much as possible," he yawned. "Damn it's been a long day."

That had to have been an understatement. I wanted to be able to tuck him into bed with a bottle and his blanket and cuddle away his stress. "Head to bed, buddy. You need sleep."

"Okay, Daddy," came his sleepy reply. "'Night 'night. Sleep well."

Derek was always sweet, but when he got tired, his little side surfaced effortlessly and it flipped that switch in me from boyfriend to Daddy. "You too, g'night."

CHAPTER 29

DEREK

Turning off my phone, I sighed and forced myself to get up off the couch before I fell asleep on it. I turned off the heater and grabbed my blanket, my thumb already going toward my mouth. As I turned around, Ty was standing at the island looking uncomfortable. I pulled my hand down quickly before it made it to my mouth and hoped like hell Ty hadn't noticed.

And that was when I noticed the open door.

Fuck. How much had he heard?

"Hey, Ty, what's up?" I forced myself to sound as calm as possible while freaking the fuck out on the inside. I was either going to have to remember to call Daddy by his name or accept the fact that everyone was going to know he was simply Daddy to me.

There seemed to be something fascinating on his thumbnail. "I need to talk to you."

I nodded. I didn't know where the conversation was going to lead, but I braced myself for uncomfortable. If Ty had heard me on the phone, he probably had all sorts of questions about my relationship. "Sunroom or kitchen?"

"Can we sit in here?" he asked me glancing nervously around the kitchen.

I was getting the impression this was *not* about me saying Daddy. The way he played with his fingernails and shuffled from foot to foot told me he was nervous. Ty had something big he needed to talk about and he was scared half to death.

"Want a drink?" I questioned as I went to the liquor cabinet and pulled out a bottle of honey whiskey. It was a little sweet for my taste, but I figured it would be more palatable to sip while we talked.

Ty nodded. "Please. On the rocks."

"Only one you're getting from me tonight. Got it? I don't think Mom will get mad if I give you one drink, any more than that and she may."

Ty nodded. "Got it. One's good anyway."

I made our drinks and set them down on the island. Standing across from him, I studied his face. He was exhausted and it looked like he was about to throw up. He took a long drink of the whiskey and set the glass down on the marble top.

Closing his eyes for a moment, he seemed to pull himself together a bit. "I-I think..." He shook his head. "No," he corrected, "I'm gay."

I had to try hard not to laugh. It was one of the biggest *duh* moments I'd had in a while. I remembered being horrified when I came out not even a year earlier and I was six years older than Ty, so I knew not to laugh. Despite how obvious his sexuality was to me, this was a big deal for him.

"Welcome to the club," I said, trying to convey sincerity and love in my voice. "Is this something you're just figuring out?"

Ty shook his head first, then shrugged. "I think I always suspected I was at least bi but these last few months, I've realized girls just don't do it for me. I was watching porn the other night and I kept staring at the guy's back and chest and his dick, thinking about how gorgeous he was. I sort of forgot there was even a woman in the room with him until I heard a breathy gasp and it totally killed it for me."

I understood that. Straight porn had never done anything for me. Before I discovered gay porn, I'd watch straight porn on mute and stare at the guy on the screen.

Gay boy problems.

"I'm here for you, Ty. You just need to ask."

Ty's eyes turned watery. "Dad's gonna hate me. Aside from demanding you go to church with us at Christmas, he hasn't said two words to you since you came out."

I leaned over the large island and squeezed Ty's hand. "Hey, the phone works both ways, Ty. I haven't called either. My feelings are hurt and I want him to come around on his own. But, if you're worried, you don't have to tell Dad at this point."

Ty drew in a shaky breath and my heart broke for him. "You aren't here. There's so much homophobia. Everywhere you turn in this town, it seems like there's someone bashing the gay community. If it isn't Pastor Tom, it's one of the coaches at the high school, or a friend's parent. I stopped speaking to a few of the guys I used to hang out with because every time we got together it was like they were trying to figure out ways to bash gays. They didn't even know about me. Everything was 'that's so gay' or 'no homo.' After hearing those things day after day, year after year, I just couldn't take it and started making excuses about why I couldn't go out with them anymore."

Ty sighed sadly. "I'm so tired of faking it, Dare. I'm gay. I *know* I'm gay, yet I can't tell anyone."

"I lived it, Ty. I knew I was gay all through high school." High school sucked, being athletic and gay was one of the hardest things I'd lived through. I had to not stare at the guys in the locker room and pray I didn't get a hard-on in front of everyone. The girls were worse, they all kept trying to get my attention and I only wanted to look at the guys. Faking it sucked.

"What about your girlfriend?"

Ty laughed. "We're friends, that's it. She knows I'm not into her like that."

"So, you've told some of your friends?" I clarified. It made me feel better knowing he hadn't had to bottle it all in like I had.

He nodded slowly. "A few. But it's hard to gauge how people are going to react."

"I get it and I didn't come out until we got the recording contract. Even then, it was by accident. But, Mom's been my biggest supporter. My band knows. And I've got an amazing boyfriend. Things seem shitty where you're at now, but they will get better. Just wait until college," I grinned.

"You've got a boyfriend?" My mom's surprised voice rang through the room, causing us both to jump.

Welcome to Coming Out: *The Marla Scott Edition.*

Mom had obviously heard us talking about Ty being gay, but she was going to focus on the fact I hadn't told her I was dating someone. Ty would spill his guts to her by the end of the night, and he would think it was on his own terms. That was just the way our mom was.

I smiled at her, "Yes, Mom. I'm dating a pretty amazing man."

Her mouth opened and I held up a hand. "Before you even ask, he's thirty-six, he's a sheriff in Tennessee, he had no clue who I was when we met, and we met in a bar. Yes, really."

"Hmm, an older man." She was quiet for a few seconds. "I think that suits you well."

My eyebrow shot up in surprise. "What the hell does that mean?"

"An older man is going to help ground you. Give you some direction. Being older and established with his career, he's going to be able to put more time and effort into your relationship. Even though his work is important, and so is yours, he's going to be able to put you first. You need that, Dare."

Damn, she's good.

"Basically," I said, running my hand over the back of my neck. She'd hit way too close to reality for my liking.

"Do you have pictures?" she asked me as she grabbed

another glass out of the cabinet. She filled her glass and topped mine off from the bottle of whiskey and took the seat beside Ty at the island.

I unlocked my phone and slid it across to them so they could see the pictures of Colt I had taken over the last week. They were mostly candid shots of him watching TV or driving, but there were a few selfies I had convinced him to take as well.

"Holy lord, Derek, your man is gorgeous," my mom said after a minute of flipping through the pictures.

"He's like sex on legs," Ty agreed.

I pulled my phone back. "Okay you two, no drooling on my new phone. That's my boyfriend."

"The sex has got to be amazing. He's got handcuffs and a Stetson," Ty said dreamily.

Mom reached over and smacked him on the back of the head playfully. "I don't care *who* you boys sleep with, but I don't need to know about your crazy sex lives."

"I think I just walked in on something I didn't want to hear," Jasper coughed.

I flipped my head to the entryway so fast my neck hurt. He was wearing work clothes and an old pair of boots. Given the late hour, he had probably been in one of the barns checking on pregnant cows and had seen the lights on in the kitchen on his way back to his house.

Jasper had been fairly cold to me since I came out. Nowhere near as bad as my dad, but enough that I didn't know how he would handle Ty coming out. And that alone made me uncomfortable.

I shrugged. "We were just talking about how hot my boyfriend is."

Jasper looked anywhere but at me. "You-you're dating someone?"

I nodded slowly. "He lives in Tennessee. We haven't been dating long, but it's pretty serious." I looked over at my mom. "We've only been dating for a few weeks. Is it too soon to be falling in love?"

She looked at me and contemplated. "It's fast, but you know your heart better than anyone else. Just make sure he's on the same page you are."

Jasper wrinkled his nose slightly.

"What?" I asked, trying not to snap, but still frustrated he was acting strange around me. "You've been weird since you found out I'm gay. Is this how it's always going to be now?"

Jasper flushed and hung his head. "I'm trying not to be weird. I'm just confused. We were taught homosexuality is a sin and then you come out and Dad isn't speaking to you and keeps telling me you're wrong... but you're my brother." His voice caught and his blue eyes were liquid. "I told you every-thing before...I miss you. I-I just want you to be happy."

The wall I had built up started to crack. "Jas, I *am* happy."

Jasper chewed on his lip and looked down at his boots. "Have you changed?" he asked the floor. The brief glance he shot me let me know he was scared and confused. I'd come out suddenly and was gone a few days later. In that time, we'd never had a chance to talk. No wonder our rela-tionship was in a weird place.

"I'm the same exact guy I've always been. I've known I liked guys since I was six. Just because you know I'm gay doesn't mean I've changed."

"What about hunting and fishing?"

It dawned on me Jasper was comparing me to every stereotype the media had thrown at us about gays—we should all be flamboyant and talk with a lisp. "I hunt, fish, and ride motorcycles because I *like* to. I've always liked it. Just because I told you I'm attracted to men doesn't change anything about me. I'm still the same guy you grew up with. And unlike your girlfriend, my boyfriend also likes hunting and fishing and dirt biking."

A weight seemed to lift off his shoulders as I spoke. "Oh. So you don't mind talking about the stuff we used to?"

I barked out a laugh. "Of course not. But if you start telling me about a hot girl, don't be offended if I start telling you about my hot boyfriend."

He studied me for a long moment before finally nodding. "Okay."

That simple word meant more to me than anything else he could have said. We had a long way to go before we were as close as we used to be, but the path was paved to get there.

We sat up talking until the horizon started turning a pinkish color. Jasper, Mom, and I had too much to drink, and Ty was tipsy. When we finally split to go to bed, my dad was already heading to the kitchen for breakfast.

CHAPTER 30

COLT

IT WAS PROBABLY UNREASONABLE, BUT I WANTED TO see Derek. It had been five days since he'd left Tennessee and we'd talked, texted, and video chatted numerous times a day, but it wasn't the same. My house felt empty without him in it.

With his relationship with Jasper being repaired by the day, Derek's mood had improved drastically. He introduced me to both of his brothers and his mom over video chat and they all, in some way or another, invited me to come to Oklahoma whenever I wanted. Derek carefully avoided the topic, always telling me he understood I had to work, but the longing in his voice told me he wanted to ask.

Wednesday morning my phone rang as I was getting ready for work.

"Good morning, buddy," I answered when I saw his face pop up on the screen.

"Hey, Daddy," Derek mumbled around a yawn. It

wasn't even eight and I was sure he'd woken up specifically to call.

"How'd you sleep last night?"

I could hear him moving around. "Pretty well. I miss you, though."

"I miss you too. But you'll be heading back this way before long."

"Is it weird I really want to play with my trains today? And have waffles for breakfast." There was a grin in his voice. He'd loved the morning I made waffles. I'd put peanut butter sauce in one part of the divided tray, maple syrup in the second, and strawberry syrup in the third. Derek had dipped, swirled, and mixed the toppings and needed a bath afterward because he'd managed to get syrup and peanut butter in his hair.

"Not at all. We'll make some time for you to play, hopefully before your next concert. Do you want me to get anything else for you or do you want to go to the store when you get here?"

"Um," he hesitated for just a beat. "Can you get me diapers?"

I was surprised at the request. We hadn't talked about them since the first day he'd stayed at my house, but I'd caught him looking at himself in the mirror enough times—running his hands over his firm bubble butt—to think he may have been curious about them. His butt was adorable no matter what was under his pants, but watching him play on the floor with a diaper filling out his pajamas was going to be perfection.

"Of course, I will. I actually already have some in your room."

"You do?" his voice was filled with surprise. "I've been wondering about them. I don't know if they will be something I'll want to use often, or ever again, but I'm curious. Do you thi—" his sentence cut off. I heard him groan, "Daddy, I need to go. Madeline's calling me."

"Have a good day, buddy."

"You too."

He clicked off and I set to work making my coffee. I had just pulled my heavy winter coat on over my uniform shirt when my phone rang again.

"Hello?" I asked, juggling my keys, Stetson, travel mug, and phone.

"I have a problem," Derek was wide awake and sounded professional. The hairs on the back of my neck stood on end and I set my stuff down giving him my full attention.

Derek took a deep breath and let it out slowly. "One of the gossip magazines got a picture of me kissing you goodbye at the airport on Saturday morning. It's clearly me. They didn't get a good shot of you, but, it's clear I'm kissing a guy."

"Fuck." *What else did I say to that?* Derek was being outed to the world and I was a ten hour drive away.

"Basically. The band agreed to a temporary contract with a management company yesterday. I haven't even met the new team yet and they want me to do a sit-down interview on Friday. Madeline agrees it's probably for the best. What do you think? Are you okay with it? What do you want me to do?"

That was a lot of information to digest. Rumors were already going to be swirling and I was glad they were giving him until Friday. I didn't listen to much radio, but I knew a country music star coming out, or being outed, was going to be huge.

"You need to do what's best for you. My life isn't in the public eye, yours is."

Derek blew out a long breath, "Now is your chance. There were no pictures where you could be identified. If, if you want out, now is the time..." his sentence trailed off.

It dawned on me what he was trying to say. "Oh, buddy. No, absolutely not. I am not leaving because people will find out about me. I'm out. I may not have announced it to the world yet, but I've been out since I was sixteen. I am an elected official, I came out to the county when I took over after the old sheriff retired. People here know. I just don't flaunt it."

Derek's voice was uneven when he finally found words. "So, y-you aren't freaking out that there's a picture of us k-kissing?"

As soon as Derek got upset, Daddy came out in full force. "Buddy, listen to me carefully. The *only* thing I'm upset about is the fact you are being forced out on someone else's schedule. I hate that your life is other people's business."

"I knew this would happen at some point," he sighed.

I pulled my coat off. "How about I fly out there today?"

"But, you have work. You were off last week. You've only been back a few days."

"Buddy, they'll survive. I'll call Zander now. His girlfriend's been driving him nuts anyway. You're more important. I'd really like to be with you right now."

Derek let out a soft laugh. "You're the best Daddy ever."

"Okay, let me go call Zander and pack.· I'll let you know my flight information."

CHAPTER 31

DEREK

Having Madeline call me at ass o'clock in the morning to tell me there were pictures of me kissing Colt was bad enough. *Seeing* the pictures she texted me was worse. It was unmistakably me. Even without the messy blonde hair, the photographer had gotten clear snaps of my face as I walked away.

The only good thing about the pictures was that they clearly weren't professional. Any paparazzo worth their salt would have, at the very least, gotten a picture of the license plate to try to track down the owner. The pictures only focused on me.

I was in shock when I called Colt back. I hadn't even told my mom about what happened, the first thought in my head was to tell Daddy everything because he would know what to do.

And he did.

He'd talked me through it and was on his way to Oklahoma. Explaining to my mom that Colt was coming and why had not been easy. There were a few moments where I worried she was going to find the publisher of the pictures and read them her version of the riot act. It took a number of tries to finally get her to understand I had been expecting this all along.

Our house was going to turn into a circus on Friday morning and there was nothing anyone could do about it. The management company wanted to send an interview crew to my parents' house. That was going to be fun to explain to my dad, but my mom assured me she would do it. While I felt like it probably should have come from me, I didn't see it going well if I told him.

Instead of worrying about my dad's reaction, I focused on the fact Daddy was coming to Oklahoma. Waiting for his plane was like waiting for Christmas morning as a kid. My mom had tried to distract me by discussing dinner ideas and had me clean the small guest house so we would have a private place to sleep.

It was her way of acknowledging we probably weren't going to be able to keep our hands off each other and she didn't want us in the house, but I was okay with that. It would give me a chance to be little again. Flannel sleep pants, my blanket, and letting my thumb slip into my mouth in bed just weren't good substitutes for my Daddy and my toys.

I was on my way to the airport before my dad was told about Colt's unexpected visit. I was glad I wasn't going to have to be there for the discussion. I didn't know how it was going to go, but I couldn't imagine it going well.

Pulling up to the airport arrival line and getting

Daddy's call saying he was waiting for his bag had my heart soaring and my nerves calming noticeably. Despite not being able to leave the truck to help him put his stuff in the back, the boy inside me began to get excited at the thought of Daddy being there. I had to remind myself I needed to drive and we had to survive the evening before we could fully escape to the guest house. Having him nearby was enough to have me calming down, some.

"How was your flight?" I asked as soon as he was seated. I wanted to lean over to kiss him so badly it hurt, but I had already been caught kissing him once at an airport and the news from Madeline that day was that the pictures were spreading like wildfire across social media.

"Uneventful, thankfully. How are you doing? Honestly." He leveled me with his stern deep voice and piercing eyes—I wouldn't have been able to lie, even if I wanted to.

The truth was easy enough anyway. "A lot better now that you're here. I'm still having a hard time wrapping my head around the fact that you came. I missed you so much but you just took time off work last week."

"Buddy, should I drive?" Daddy asked as I rambled.

I shook my head. "I'm good. Just excited you're here."

"I can tell, you've been practically vibrating in your seat."

"I want to kiss you and hug you, but we're in public and Madeline may kill me if I get another picture taken of us kissing before Friday."

He squeezed my leg and it helped settle me down. "You can kiss me when we get to your house. Until then, focus on driving or I'm going to have you pull over so I can."

By the time we got back to my parents' house, it was well past lunch and Ty would likely be home from school any minute. I drove around back to the guest house and parked. "My mom basically told me we're staying out here for the weekend."

I opened the door so we could set his stuff down. "This is perfect," Colt said as he leaned over to give me a kiss. "It gives us our own space so you can play tonight or tomorrow morning. I brought some of your stuff with me."

My eyes widened. "You did? What did you bring?"

I may have bounced. I missed playing with my toys and being Daddy's boy. It should have shocked me how quickly my life had changed, yet it felt right. Like coming home and being wrapped up in a big warm blanket. Only my big warm blanket was actually my security blanket, my thumb, my toys, and my Daddy.

"When we have time, buddy. For now, shouldn't we go say hello to your family?"

I pouted. "Yes, Daddy. Warning, Ty's going to be home and he and my mom are going to pepper you with questions."

Daddy just chuckled and shook his head. "Well, let's get this over with then."

I reached over and grabbed his hand as we headed back to the house. As we reached the back deck I stopped and gave him a kiss. "Just remember, they're nuts."

I didn't know what I'd find when I opened the door to the house. There could be silence, or the house could be filled to the brim with people. I opened the door to my mom standing at the kitchen sink and Declan and Ty sitting at the kitchen island with school books spread out in front of them, the sides of their bodies pressed against one another as they worked. I rolled my eyes at them. It had become clear they were oblivious to how affectionate they were with each other.

"Hey guys," I said entering the kitchen. "This is my boyfriend, Colt Westfield. Colt, this is my mom, Marla, my brother, Ty, and his best friend, Declan." I pointed to each one in turn and watched as Ty's mouth fell open.

"It's so nice to finally meet you!" My mom pulled Colt into a tight hug like he was a long lost child, not her son's new boyfriend.

When he was finally able to break free, he seemed a little red, likely from lack of oxygen.

"Take a seat, I'm just starting dinner," Mom said as she waved her spoon toward the island.

Ty had been staring at us since we walked in. Declan couldn't pass up the opportunity to rib him a bit when he grabbed the napkin off the stack in the center of the island. "Hey, dude, you've got a little drool there." He handed the napkin over to Ty. "Remember, he's taken."

"I do not." He bumped Declan with his shoulder, but his face flushed.

We pulled stools up to the island and talked as my mom made dinner. Colt volunteered information about his family, and mine were, blessedly, well-behaved. There had been no awkward childhood stories, or embarrassing

CHAPTER 32

COLT

As Marla was pulling the roast and rolls out of the oven, I noticed Derek's dad heading in with, a guy I could only assume was, Derek's older brother. Derek's back went rigid and nervous energy radiated off him. I placed a hand on his thigh and squeezed.

"Calm down, buddy. It will be okay."

"He hasn't spoken to me in months because I'm gay. I knew that when you met it would be stressful, but this is harder than I expected."

Ty leaned over and gave Derek a hug which seemed to relax him some.

"It smells amazing in here," the large, gray-haired man said as he walked into the house. Brice Scott was as tall as Derek and held himself in an intimidating manner that made me understand why Derek was uneasy around him.

The younger blonde, who looked so similar to Derek I knew he had to be Jasper, also inhaled deeply. "Roast! My favorite."

"You know you have your own house equipped with a fully functioning kitchen, right?" Ty mentioned. "I had to help move the appliances in there. Have you ever even turned on the stove?"

"Actually, yes. I've made hot chocolate a few times this winter," Jasper said with a grin as he glanced over at the island and noticed Derek and me sitting next to Ty. "Oh, hey, Mom said you were coming. Sorry, I managed to lose track of time and didn't realize you'd be here already. I'm Jasper." He held out his hand and I took it.

"Nice to meet you. I'm Colt."

Derek's dad looked over at the island and his eyes flashed with surprise. Derek said his dad knew I would be there, but I wondered if that was actually the case. Derek's knee jerked hard under my hand. I was about to suggest we head back to the guest house when Brice found his words.

Brice forced a smile and nodded his head toward me. "Hello, Colt."

"Guys, go clean up. Dinner will be ready when you get back," Marla stated from her spot in front of the stove, dismissing the two quickly.

"What can us lazy bums do to help with dinner?" I asked from my place at the island. I was still rubbing Derek's leg and was starting to feel some of his tension dissipating.

"Set the table and get everyone drinks," Marla instructed.

We jumped up and began grabbing plates, glasses, and silverware. We spent five minutes setting the table, then another five running casserole dishes and bowls of food to the dining room to help prepare for dinner. By the time Jasper and Brice returned, the dining room was ready. We all found places around the table and began to pass dishes.

"So, Colt," Brice said casually, though I could tell how hard he was working to keep his voice that way. "What is it you do for a living?"

I smiled politely. "I'm the sheriff of a small area outside of Nashville."

The admission seemed to intrigue Brice because he relaxed and looked at me curiously. "And how long have you been the sheriff?"

"Almost three years now. I took over when the previous sheriff retired suddenly, but I was elected just over two years ago."

Brice seemed to accept the answer and nodded. He didn't have much else to say to us throughout dinner, but at least he didn't look as frustrated at my presence as he had before. I kept catching Brice's curious glances throughout the meal and I couldn't quite figure them out.

I kept a hand on Derek's thigh and occasionally reached behind him to rub his mid-back inconspicuously. The touches calmed him and he slowly began to relax.

As soon as dinner was over, Brice pushed back from the table and looked at Jasper. "Let's go over the numbers." Jasper seemed annoyed at the order and shot Derek an apologetic glance as he followed Brice from the room.

Derek sagged into my arms. "That was intense."

I had to agree with him. There hadn't been any open hostility, but Brice hadn't welcomed me with open arms either. I was impressed he had managed to ask me two questions. I only wished he had extended the same courtesy to his son.

"We help Mom with the dishes while Dad and Jasper talk business. It's sort of a tradition."

I picked up my plate and followed Derek into the kitchen. By the time we'd arrived, the radio had been turned on, Marla was rinsing off plates, while Ty and Declan put leftovers into containers. Ty was singing along to the radio and Derek joined in while he put dishes into the dishwasher. Between the noise of the radio, the singing and talking, and the clattering of the dishes, I wondered how Jasper and Brice were able to discuss work.

As the song changed, Marla's eyes widened and she turned the radio up. Derek laughed and bumped her shoulder. "Ma, if you want me to sing a song, just ask, you don't have to deafen us with the radio."

"Then sing this one, I love it." She handed over a whisk and Derek laughed, but grabbed it like he would a microphone.

I watched him dance around the kitchen while singing Hometown's latest single into the whisk. There was a short break in singing and Derek danced over to kiss me. What started as a brief peck quickly turned deeper as his mom, Ty, and Declan began to clap and cheer. By the time we pulled apart, Derek's lips were kiss swollen and he had to gasp in a breath before catching up with the song.

Glancing toward the doorway, I saw Brice standing there watching our shenanigans. I hoped I wasn't reading too much into it, but he definitely seemed more thoughtful than angry or uncomfortable. He turned to leave before anyone else noticed him watching.

As the song ended, Derek put the whisk away in the proper drawer. "It's still really weird to hear my voice on the radio, but especially on the station I grew up listening to."

"Then we won't tell you about what a big deal they make every time a new single comes out," Ty giggled.

Marla shook her head. "Grab a few beers and we'll head to the living room. Your dad and Jasper should be done with their *meeting* and if they aren't, well, they're going to be now."

Derek and I each grabbed a six-pack and headed toward the living room.

Brice and Jasper were finishing up a discussion about birthing season as we walked in.

"Thank you," Jasper practically purred as Derek handed him a beer. "So, Mom said you're coming out publicly," he mentioned after a long pull from his bottle.

I settled myself onto the couch and Derek curled into my side so tightly my arm had no choice but to wrap around him. "Well, technically I'm being outted," he started uncomfortably. "There's pictures of me kissing this one." He patted my chest and smiled. "I have to address them and it's going to be easier to come out than deny it."

It sounded logical and reasonable, but the way his body tensed in my arms, I knew he wasn't as calm as he was letting on.

"What is the plan, then?" Jasper asked.

Derek shrugged. "There's going to be an interview

crew coming here Friday. This place is going to be a zoo for a few hours."

"Here?" Jasper's eyebrows shot up in surprise.

Derek chewed his lip and nodded. "Yeah, sorry."

"I'm sorry, Dare. It sucks it's such a big deal," Jasper said sincerely.

The topics shifted to lighter things and Derek spent an hour or so telling more stories from the tour while I shared some stories from my time as sheriff. We had finished the beers and it was starting to get late.

I could tell Derek was ready to call it a night. His thumb had been creeping toward his mouth and he had almost called me Daddy twice.

"Why don't we head out? I think you're tired."

Derek gave a sharp nod. "I am."

CHAPTER 33

DEREK

THE BRIGHT SIDE OF GETTING THE GUEST CABIN READY earlier in the day was that my blanket was on the bed when we got back.

"Climb up on the bed, I'll be there in just a minute," Daddy told me as the door shut behind us.

I listened to him in the kitchen. I heard the water run and the fridge open and shut, but I didn't think much of it. I had my blanket, my thumb was in my mouth, and my brain was starting to quiet down after the chaos of the day.

My brain had turned the request into a command that let me know I could finally let go. Daddy would take care of me. When he came into the room with a sippy cup for me, I didn't even think about it as I took it and put it to my lips.

He bent down and dug through the larger of the two suitcases he'd brought with him. He pulled out a gray outfit —pajamas, maybe—that had blue trim and smiling little fuzz-balls and snaps down the front. It was one of the clothing items I hadn't worn yet, but the bright pattern had drawn my attention a number of times. My feet started wiggling back and forth as I waited for him to get me dressed.

"Is someone excited?" Daddy questioned.

I hadn't noticed I was smiling around the cup until my cheeks were suddenly sore from grinning. I nodded around the spout. Daddy had given me apple juice and words weren't worth giving up the juice.

He bent down and stood back up with something else in his hand. It had bright, colorful swirls on it so it took me a moment to realize Daddy was holding a diaper. My eyes widened and I opened my mouth, breaking the seal I had on the spout and causing a rush of air to enter.

"D-diaper?" I almost whispered. The little bit of my adult brain that was still firing was screaming for me to stop but my body was vibrating with curiosity. I wanted to try it. I'd been curious for a few weeks and now there was a diaper not even three feet from me.

And I could wear it.

"You said you wanted to try them earlier today. Do you still want to?" he asked.

I nodded before my big brain could convince me otherwise. My little brain was *loving* the idea of diapers. I could already feel blood rushing south and my cock filling. While I was new to age play, it had been on my radar—even if I refused to entertain it—long enough that I knew I wanted to try diapers as soon as they were brought up the first time. To think it was finally going to happen wasn't even overwhelming, it just felt... right.

"Sit up so we can start getting all these layers off." Daddy held out his hands and I took them while he gently tugged me so I was seated on the edge of the bed.

My mom had complained the bed was taller than she had expected when it came in, but the way my feet didn't touch the ground helped me slip further into my little headspace.

I swung my feet and tried to point my toes so they touched the floor, but I was unsuccessful. Daddy tugged at the hem of my sweatshirt and I lifted my arms above my head. Once the sweatshirt was off, he repeated the process with my t-shirt. Despite having the heat on, I shivered as cold air touched my warm skin.

Daddy grabbed the throw blanket off the chair and covered my shoulders and back with it and I wrapped the edges around me so they covered my chest as well. "Time to get your pants off too," he announced before going for the button, popping it open and sliding the zipper down.

He placed his hands on my biceps and helped me slide off the bed until my feet touched the floor. As soon as I was standing, my jeans slipped off my hips and pooled at my feet leaving me in just a pair of emerald green briefs.

"It's a good thing we ordered you better undies for little time," Daddy said with a laugh before hooking his fingers in the waistband and pulling them down my legs.

The cold air hit my dick and balls and my erection flagged drastically.

"Well, it'll be easier to get a diaper on you when you aren't hard as a rock," Daddy laughed as he helped me step out of the fabric puddled at my feet.

With the statement, my body got confused. My dick wanted to get hard at the thought of wearing a diaper for the first time, but the air was cold enough that it was only twitching slightly in response.

"Up on the bed before you freeze."

I turned around and tried to climb onto the bed still holding the blanket tightly around me. The attempt was awkward and had to look even more clumsy than it felt. Daddy finally gave me a gentle push on the backside while laughing at me.

"Buddy, it isn't *that* cold in here. You're going to have to lose the blanket so Daddy can get you ready for bed." I grumbled my disagreement, but let go of the blanket. He rewarded me with a smile.

I watched as he reached for the diaper sitting beside me on the bed. I hadn't paid much attention to it before that point, but now that it was in his hand, I couldn't take my eyes off it. *Would it be soft? How thick would it be? Was I going to like it?* I must have gotten lost in my thoughts because he was between my legs smiling at me. "Lift up, buddy," Daddy told me. The amused tone in his voice told me he had asked more than once.

Oops.

I pushed my hips into the air and let him adjust the diaper under me. I must have been more nervous than I thought because my cock was still soft.

Daddy gave my hip a light pat. "Back down." I slowly lowered my butt to the diaper. It didn't feel like much just laying under my ass. Taking a few calming breaths, I finally looked up.

"What do you think, buddy? Do you want to play with blocks some, or watch TV until you're ready for bed?"

My eyes lit up. "You brought my blocks?"

Daddy had my diaper smoothed over my stomach and was working on securing the tape on the left side, but was still able to easily carry on a conversation with me.

"I brought your blocks and a few of your trains. You can choose what you want to play with."

"Trains, Daddy," I announced with all the certainty in the world.

Daddy pulled the last tape shut and adjusted the leak guards by running his finger lightly along the inside edge of the diaper.

My diaper.

I stared down at it for a long minute before Daddy finally pulled me out of my thoughts. "Ready for your pajamas?"

"The fuzz-ball things?" I questioned. I still couldn't decide what to call them, but they were cute.

"They are small fuzzy monsters, I think. But yes, those."

I nodded and explored my diaper some. First I touched the plastic outer shell and found it to be softer than I'd expected, but the loud crinkle every time I shifted my hips was unmistakable. Squeezing my legs together had my dick waking up. The material bunched up and pushed against my crotch making me feel snug and confined but also aroused. My dick finally started to swell, a strange feeling within the confines of the cotton batting. I rocked my hips up to see how it would feel and a light moan escaped me.

That felt good.

"Buddy," Daddy said in exasperation. "When you're little, you don't play with yourself, remember?"

I nodded, I remembered the rule, but with a diaper between my legs it was going to be harder to follow. I wiggled around wondering what the different movements would feel like.

"Buddy," Daddy warned, but there was laughter in his voice and his eyes were sparkling.

"Sorry, Daddy."

He unfolded the pajamas that turned out to be a one piece cotton sleeper with snaps up both legs and straight up the stomach. "If you can't stop rubbing yourself, Daddy is going to have to make it so you *can't* get to it, is that what you want?"

"Uh." Daddy *was* talking about a cock cage, *right*? What was the right answer? I couldn't decide, but the thought made me sit still and wait for the next instruction.

"I think my boy likes that idea. I'm going to have to remember that in the future. But for now, we have to get your pj's on. With the snaps on the legs, I'll be able to get your diaper changed without having to get you totally undressed," Daddy explained.

I liked that idea, especially with it being so cold.

"For tonight, though, we can just unsnap the top buttons and pull them up your legs." He knelt down in front of me and helped guide my legs into each hole. My feet felt the cotton material encase them and I couldn't help the surprised giggle that escaped me at the sensation.

"My boy likes his footies," Daddy said as he guided the

pajamas up my thighs. "Okay, you're going to have to stand up so I can get you fully dressed."

I slid off the bed and let Daddy guide both of my arms into the sleeper then waited patiently as he snapped it closed. In under a minute I had gone from wearing only a diaper to wearing a snug fitting sleeper that clearly showed off my puffy diaper.

I liked it.

"Thank you, Daddy," I said as I leaned toward him to give him a kiss.

Daddy smiled. "You're very welcome, buddy. Do you want your trains now?"

Tapping my finger to my chin, I thought for a moment. "Trains *and* blocks!"

Daddy laughed. "Alright, go on out to the living room, I'll be out with your toys."

CHAPTER 34

COLT

Derek was lost in his own world as he played with his toys. I pushed the coffee table to the side when I got them out to let him spread out on the floor. It wasn't as nice as my living room where he had plenty of space to crawl around, but he hadn't seemed to mind.

Laying on his stomach, his pajamas pulled tightly across his backside accentuated the diaper wrapped around him. Aside from an occasional wiggle, either to get friction on his dick or to just adjust himself, I wasn't quite sure which, he didn't seem to notice it was there. Once he was diapered, though, he seemed to sink further into his little headspace than he had before.

Derek's thumb had been in his mouth for most of the last hour. He was pushing the trains around with little sounds and giggling as he played. After playing for almost ninety minutes, I noticed that Derek had gone quiet. A quick glance down proved he had curled himself into a ball and was drifting off to sleep.

"Hey buddy, let's go get into bed and you can have a bottle before you fall asleep on the floor."

Derek mumbled something around his thumb that could have been either an agreement or a protest. I stood up and patted the diaper that was sticking up and he groaned, wiggling his butt slightly but making no move to get up. I went to the kitchen and filled a bottle halfway with milk. There was no way he'd make it through a full bottle, but when he was little he liked to have a bottle and a story before bed. My boy was already snoring softly, his right thumb in his mouth, a train car in his left hand. If the floor wasn't so cold, I'd have left him there, but I knew by morning he'd be miserable.

"Bedtime, buddy," I told him while rubbing his back.

Derek groaned and stretched, the diaper crinkling under him.

"Now, buddy. I have your bottle and the train book's in our room."

That was what Derek needed to get him motivated to move and he finally got up, leaving the train car on the floor. He took my hand with his left hand and followed me to the bedroom. A quick glance over my shoulder found him waddling slightly, not used to the bulk between his legs.

So. Fucking. Adorable.

As soon as we were in the bed, Derek flopped across my lap, his head resting on a stack of pillows beside me. "What train book did you bring, Daddy?" he asked before I slipped the nipple into his mouth.

"The one that makes the noise at the end."

I got halfway through the book before he was asleep. It took a few minutes to get him to his side of the bed. As he settled into his pillows he sighed. "Night, Daddy."

I could have sworn I had just closed my eyes when I woke up to Derek grinding against my hip. I cracked one eye open and looked at my boy who was chasing all the friction he could get. His pupils were blown wide and he was letting out soft whimpers of pleasure.

"Do you want something?" I teased.

Derek nodded and thrust into my hip again, the crinkle of the diaper loud in the quiet room. He groaned and threw his arm over his eyes. "Ugh, diaper. That's awkward."

I pulled his arm away from his eyes and kissed his forehead. "No. It's sexy as fuck. I don't care if you're little or not, I will always find the sight of you in a diaper sexy."

Even in the dim light, I could see a blush spread across his face. "If you say so."

"I do say so," I replied as I pushed him gently onto his back so I could work on getting him out of his pajamas and diaper. He seemed to understand how useful the snapping pajamas were when I was able to get him stripped without ever having him stand up. I tossed them off the bed and turned my attention to his diaper.

Derek's cock sprang free as soon as I had the second tape unfastened. It had been straining against his diaper and judging by the string of precum stretched between his slit and the diaper as I pulled it away, he was probably closer to cumming than I'd realized.

He bucked his hips into the air chasing any pleasure he

could find. "Patience," I murmured as I wadded the dry diaper up and threw it away.

"Need... you... now," he panted.

I dropped to my knees beside the bed and ran my tongue from the crease of his ass up to his balls. I felt Derek tense and he cried out as my tongue passed over his hole.

"Daaaaddy," Derek whined. "Fuck me, please!" he begged as his hand went to his dick. I was still surprised to find being called Daddy during sex didn't bother me.

"So impatient," I hummed. "Don't touch." I ducked my head again and dragged my tongue back toward his hole. When I reached it, I pushed my tongue in briefly before moving back up to his balls. The power I felt listening to him moan and watching him writhe on the bed, trying to not touch his cock was heady. Knowing he was listening, trying to please me, made me want to give him everything.

Before I got too lost in my head, I ran my tongue down to his hole again, tongue fucking him and loosening his ring of muscle. It only took a minute before I knew Derek wouldn't be able to take more. His pleas had already become wordless babbling. If I continued, he was likely to cum before I was inside him and that was not what I wanted.

"Ung," he moaned at the loss of contact as I leaned up to grab the lube. I was happy I'd stuck a bottle of lube and a few condoms on the nightstand as I unpacked. A short reach, and both were in my hand.

I put the condom on quickly. He was so desperate already I didn't want to make him wait after he'd been stretched. The snick of the lube bottle seemed louder than normal in the quiet room and Derek was so aroused the squelching sound as I poured lube onto my hand had him gasping. I didn't know if he was going to be able to hold off until I had him stretched enough to enter him. It was a good thing he didn't like a lot of prep.

I pushed two fingers into him, making sure his channel was slick while I rubbed my cock with the excess on my other hand. Derek's hips pushed against my fingers, chasing all the pleasure he could get and I knew he was ready.

Lining up with his entrance, I slid in with one long stroke. Above me, Derek's fists beat against the mattress and grabbed at the sheets. When my balls hit his ass, I moved his legs up, pushing his knees toward his chest.

"Please. Please. Please," he was almost chanting once his body had adjusted to me inside of him. "More. Faster." Full sentences had eluded him well before that moment and all he had left were whimpers and single words.

I pulled almost completely out and slammed back into him, not being slow or gentle.

I couldn't help the moan that escaped my lips when Derek reached for his thighs to pull his legs back. The action rocked his hips upward and I could feel my cock slide deeper into him. The new angle allowed Derek's prostate to be nailed with each thrust and precum leaked from his cock as I fucked him.

"Daddy. Ungh. Gonna. Can't. Need," he gasped.

My orgasm was barreling down on me and I didn't have long. I wrapped my hand around his leaking cock and began to stroke him rapidly. Derek didn't tell me to stop, instead, his hips thrust upward as he called out. I was thankful we were a good distance from the house. Between his screams and the headboard thudding against the wall with every thrust, the entire house would have been awake by now.

I only had a few thrusts left before I came and somehow managed to grit out, "Cum."

The word barely passed my lips when Derek's body tightened and ropes of white cum shot upward, painting his chest and abs. The pulsation of his ass, pulling me even farther into him, pushed me over the edge and my orgasm crashed through me. My hips stuttered then stilled and I groaned as I filled the condom. "Fuck, baby," I panted as the last waves subsided.

His chest was rising and falling rapidly as he fought to catch his breath. I leaned forward, my cock still in his ass, while I licked one of the stripes of cum off his chest. It had painted his caramel nipple and he hissed as my tongue glided over it. The combination of sweat coating his chest and the salty, slightly sweet, cum on my tongue was almost enough to get me hard again—*almost*. After that powerful orgasm, it was probably going to be a while before I was good for anything but sleep.

I slowly pulled out and headed toward the bathroom. I needed to get myself cleaned up and get a rag to clean Derek up. I found two clean washcloths in the closet and used one to clean myself off and took the second back out to where Derek was still lying on the bed with a totally debauched look on his face. I wiped him off gently and he smiled.

"You ok, buddy?" I asked as I folded the washcloth and set it aside. I glanced at the clock on the nightstand and saw it was only 3:30 in the morning.

"So, so good," Derek replied sleepily.

I laid back down beside him and pulled him against me, nuzzling my face into his hair. I was glad we had more time to sleep and recover. As much as Derek needed time to be little, I needed time to be his Daddy. Even though what we had just done had nothing to do with Derek's little side, my Daddy side still craved the closeness of cuddling my boy. I drifted off to sleep again with him held tightly in my arms.

When we woke in the morning, Derek was wrapped around me. He had his left arm flung across my chest while his right arm was tucked between us, holding his blanket, his thumb in his mouth. His left leg was draped over my legs. I couldn't remember a moment when I had ever been happier. I looked at my boy and smiled before gently shifting, there was no way to move without waking him up. Derek's eyes opened slowly and he blinked up at me.

"G'morning, Daddy," he murmured around his thumb.

"Good morning, buddy," I responded reaching out to brush a sleep-mussed curl from his forehead. "Are you ready to start the day?"

"No..." Derek grumbled pulling his thumb from his mouth and covering his head with his blanket.

I laughed and tugged playfully on the blanket. "Come

on, buddy. I'm sure you're probably hungry." As I finished the sentence, Derek's stomach rumbled. "See, I told you."

We took our time showering and getting ready for the day before finally heading toward the main house for breakfast. Derek held my hand and talked about whatever came to his mind on the short walk. It was cold and we walked briskly through the field, our long legs quickly eating up the distance.

I opened the door and put my hand on the small of Derek's back to usher him inside. The smell of fresh waffles wafted out the open door and Derek's eyes lit up. "Waffles, Daddy!" He did a little hop step and bounced into the kitchen. I heard someone sputter and begin choking.

Derek blushed and buried his face into my shoulder. I wrapped my arm around his back and held him for a moment while scanning the room to see who was in the kitchen.

Ty was the only one and he was trying to clean coffee off the cabinets and counter. As soon as he was satisfied, he quirked his eyebrow at his brother, the same way Derek did when he found something fascinating. Judging by the look in Ty's eyes, Derek had become the most fascinating thing on his radar.

I hoped the look I sent Ty as I ushered Derek to the island was enough to keep him quiet. Marla had set out trays and pans of food, a stack of plates, and glasses of juice on the massive island.

"There are two types of syrup," Derek said to me quietly.

"Do you want them both?"

Derek nodded. "But they're going to mix on my plate and get my waffle soggy." His face scrunched up like he'd bit into a lemon and was staring at the syrup and his plate like an answer would jump out at him.

Ty was watching the two of us with rapt attention. He didn't care if he was staring, he wanted to know what was up with us, but I forced myself to ignore his stares.

"Okay, are there small bowls or containers around here?" I asked him.

While Derek thought about it, Ty turned and reached into a lower cabinet and produced two small containers that wouldn't hold more than a few ounces each.

"Perfect. Thanks." I smiled at Ty as I set them on Derek's plate. "Now you have something to hold your syrup and they won't mix or make your waffle soggy."

Derek smiled like he'd just won the lottery. "Awesome."

Ty nodded. "Yeah... you have the perfect Daddy." His eyes were sparkling with amusement. I didn't detect any malice in his tone or his expression so I let it slide.

Derek blushed red and fumbled with the bottle of maple syrup.

"Behave, Ty," I told him as I took the syrup out of Derek's hand to pour it into the container.

"Only through breakfast. After that, though, it's on."

Derek groaned and leaned back against me. I kissed his temple. "Go sit down, I'll make up your plate before you end up dropping it."

"Thank you," he muttered before turning and grabbing

one of the glasses of juice. The way his hands trembled as he grabbed it, I hoped he made it to the dining room without spilling it.

I turned my attention back to his plate, cutting up the waffles. It was normal for me to cut food up for Derek. I did it at home, even when he wasn't little, and he always seemed to appreciate it.

Ty snorted a giggle. "Oh, you guys are so much more intriguing than I would have ever guessed!"

I shook my head in amusement. "Behave yourself, Ty."

"Oh, I'll be good... through breakfast. I already told you that."

I took my plate and Derek's to the dining room and sat down.

CHAPTER 35

DEREK

I BLINKED A FEW TIMES WHEN THE PLATE OF WAFFLES and sausage was placed in front of me, both items cut into bite-sized pieces and the different syrups in the small bowls. I tried to fight the blush creeping up my face and glanced nervously around the room to see who else noticed.

My dad and Jasper were talking about a calf born early that morning on the cattle side of the ranch. My mom was listening to Declan tell her about a school project he'd been working on and didn't do much more than glance in our direction and give a smile of acknowledgment. Ty, on the other hand was openly gawking at me, the wheels were turning so fast in his head they were almost audible.

I finally managed to get myself calmed down enough that I felt like I was able to pick up my juice and get it to my mouth without risk of spilling it when Ty leaned over. "Submission looks good on you."

I sputtered and coughed but managed to not spit my

drink across the dining room. "Are you trying to kill me?" I hissed.

"Are you going to try to deny it?" he smirked.

I stabbed a waffle cube with my fork. "You said you'd behave through breakfast," I whispered.

Ty laughed, glanced around to make sure no one was paying attention to us and leaned in close to my ear. "I knew sex with your man would be hot as hell."

Colt heard and tried to cover his laugh with a cough, while simultaneously reaching over and smacking Ty on the back of the head. My brother was killing me. He was obviously more versed in alternative lifestyles than I had ever imagined. Christ, I was still figuring out I was a little and I was six years older than him. It was going to be a long morning.

Thankfully, we got through the rest of breakfast without incident. "Do you want me to talk to Ty with you?" Daddy questioned as he gathered our plates.

Yes!

Maybe.

No.

I shook my head. "I'm good, but I might as well get this over with."

"Only tell him what you're comfortable with," Daddy reminded me. "I'm going to help your mom clean up the dishes so you guys have some time to talk."

I nodded and gave him a quick kiss. "Hey, Ty, let's go talk for a minute," I said, proud of how casual I sounded.

"Sure, lead the way," he said with a smirk toward

Declan. those two knew each other too well, because Declan gave him a knowing wink.

Ty bounded into my room and plopped himself down in my desk chair. I barely had the door shut and hadn't even made it to my bed when he started in about what he'd witnessed. "*Daddy?*" he questioned, excitement practically bubbling out of him.

"Ty," I warned.

He didn't stop though. "No seriously, you called Colt Daddy. And he cut your breakfast up for you like it was nothing. *Ohmygod*," he gasped. "You're a little!"

My face went red, but I couldn't deny it. I could, however, end his rambling. "Whoa, Ty, stop." I took a deep breath when he finally clamped his mouth shut. "I've always had a thing for older men, and, yes, I like the Daddy/boy dynamic. It just so happens Colt is a fairly dominant guy and when we first met, he was able to read me like a book."

Ty turned serious. "Dare, are you okay with the lifestyle? He's not forcing you into something you're not comfortable with, is he? BDSM is serious stuff. There is a lot of trust that goes into that type of relationship. If you aren't completely on board with what is going on, you're destined for failure."

I put my hand up to stop him. I was touched by his concern for me and for my emotions. "Ty, I'm good. In practice, it's new to me, and even though it's not new to Colt, it's the first time he's been in a serious relationship like this. He hasn't forced me into anything, I promise." I stopped, not sure how much I should divulge about our relationship.

Ty continued like this was a normal conversation for a weekday morning, "There are a lot of ways that the Daddy/boy fantasy plays out. Hell, sometimes it is just Daddy being, well Daddy. He makes decisions, he punishes appropriately—for some that is orgasm denial or control for others it may be spankings or canings." I couldn't stop the cringe on my face when Ty mentioned canings. "And apparently that part isn't for you," he said with a laugh.

"Uh, no, definitely not canes, or whips, or paddles. Spankings can be hot, but nothing more severe."

Ty looked thoughtful and seemed to agree when he nodded slightly. "So, how little are you?" he asked. There was no judgment or repulsion on his face or in his voice.

I shrugged, pretending we weren't talking about fetishes. "Little." I'd let him decide how little that actually was.

Ty smiled at me and I could tell that he was working something through in his head. "Do you enjoy it?"

I nodded without much thought. "Yeah. It's nice. My brain shuts off. I get to watch cartoons and play with toys and have a bottle or a sippy cup." I didn't even bother trying to hide my blush.

I was talking about age play with my brother! How much fucking weirder could my day get?

"If your Daddy is okay with it, you should try diapers. I think you'd like them."

My mouth hung open. Not only had Ty referred to

Colt as my Daddy, but he brought up diapers like they were an everyday thing. I pulled my shoulders up and rocked my head from side to side, not sure how to tell him diapers were already part of our play.

Ty sat up straighter in the desk chair, his eyes wide with knowledge. "You've already tried them! You like them, don't you?"

And the day just got much weirder... Fucking hell we were actually talking about diapers.

"You love giving up that control," Ty stated like it all made sense. I got the impression he was talking to himself, especially after he continued before giving me a chance to respond. "You have one of the most demanding jobs I can think of. You are always in the spotlight and have to be 'on' whenever you're out of the house. You need something to help you relax. Being little gives you the break you need, right?"

Instead of answering him, I decided to ask a question, "Who the hell are you? And what did you do with the cute little kid who used to follow me around?"

Ty grinned wickedly. "Don't let my innocent face fool you. I've got secrets, I just hide them better than you apparently." He winked at me. "Besides, life would be pretty boring without a kink or two. Come on, let's go find your Daddy. He's probably about to worry himself sick that you and I are up here and he has no idea what's going on."

I laughed. "You're probably right. Also, watch what you call him around other people. I *may* be okay with you saying he's my Daddy when it's just us, but no one else noticed and I don't want them to notice, either."

"Your secret is safe with me. Now the real question is, are you still my big brother, or are you my baby brother now?" I would have crawled under the bed in embarrassment if he wasn't grinning in obvious playfulness. Instead, I took the opportunity to smack him on the back of the head as we left my room.

As we headed out, I heard Declan yell that they were going to be late for school. Ty ran to his room to grab his bag and I headed to the kitchen. Ty's shirt caught on his bag for a brief second as he skidded through the kitchen and I could have sworn I saw a blue silk-looking top under his black shirt. I didn't have time to process it though because Daddy was at my side.

"Everything go okay, buddy?" he asked quietly.

I nodded and leaned into him for a hug. As the front door shut, it dawned on me I never asked Ty what kinky shit he was into.

Damn.

CHAPTER 36

COLT

THERE WAS A KNOCK ON THE CABIN DOOR AT 6:45 Friday morning. "What the hell?" Derek mumbled around his thumb. He was wearing a pair of pajamas and a diaper I had put him in before bed.

He rolled out of bed and headed to the door still holding his blanket with his thumb in his mouth. "Buddy, wait up. Let me answer it." Derek was going to give the person at the door quite a shock if he opened it dressed like that.

I slipped out of bed, thankful I'd fallen asleep in my flannel pants. They were loose and hung low on my hips, but at least I was fully covered and a glance behind me told me Derek didn't mind the view.

"It's Madeline," I called as I reached the front door.

He groaned. "What is she doing here so early? Let her in, Daddy. She's seen me through the front door by now and she's going to throw a fit if we don't get the door opened soon. She's not dressed for this weather."

He wasn't wrong. Madeline's black slacks and white silk top were no match for the cold wind whipping across the fields that morning. It didn't matter that she was wearing a wool peacoat, she was going to be cold, especially since she hadn't bothered to button it.

Her eyes were wide when I finally got the door open. "What the... you know what, I don't want to know," she amended.

"Thankfully, *you* signed an NDA," Derek snarked.

Madeline shook her head. "I really wish you'd let Colt sign one." She looked at Derek again and muttered, "Especially now that I know *way* more than I wanted to about your personal life."

"Hey, you showed up here unannounced at 6:45 in the morning."

"You will always get a call from now on."

I scoffed. "I'd have *thought* you'd have learned to do that after walking in on us fucking in the hotel room."

She shook her head. "School of hard knocks, apparently. Your mom was kind enough to send me with breakfast for us."

She set down three containers of food on the small counter and glanced over at Derek again letting her eyes fall to the puffiness at his midsection.

Each container held identical breakfasts containing eggs, bacon, and pancakes. The Scott men burned a lot of calories working on the ranch each day, and Marla's meals were meant to keep them going. It also meant there was no way Madeline or I would be able to finish our meals. From the way Derek's stomach growled when he smelled the food, I didn't put it past him to finish the entire thing.

I opened a container and passed it to Madeline then opened mine. Derek's breakfast was notable because it had been sent in a divided container—eggs in one smaller compartment, bacon in the other, and pancakes in the largest section. I chuckled when I saw the two containers of syrup in Derek's tray. Marla had clearly noticed Derek's breakfast the day before. I wondered how much else she'd noticed.

Madeline watched with wide eyes as I cut up Derek's pancakes. He hadn't made a move to change his pajamas and was standing against the counter in his blue train-print pajama bottoms and a white shirt with blue sleeves. The shirt had a large train on the front with the words "I choo-choose Daddy" written in smoke above the smokestack.

"Thanks, Daddy," Derek said as I handed over his container.

"This takes *Daddy* to a whole new level. You know that, right?" Madeline asked as she stabbed a bite of pancake.

Derek grinned. "NDA. Also, you showed up at some ungodly hour. If you show up before sun up, I'm probably going to look something like this." He shrugged at her exasperated sigh.

Madeline shook her head. "I can't say I *understand* it, but I can accept it. Your secret's safe with me, but you'd better get changed after breakfast because Harrison is coming over. He'll be here around 7:30."

Derek's head cocked to the side. "Why's Harrison coming over?"

"Uh, he's your best friend and he wanted to be here for the interview. Let's be honest here, Derek. There is something going on between Harrison and Neil. You coming out is either going to convince Harrison it's okay to come out, or it's going to push him further into the closet."

"Ugh, no pressure or anything, though." Derek grumbled.

CHAPTER 37

DEREK

By 8:15, THE HOUSE WAS PACKED. HARRISON HAD shown up at the guest house at 7:25, narrowly avoiding seeing me in the training pants Daddy surprised me with after my shower. I'd had no idea they'd arrived that week or that they made it to Oklahoma with him. Of course, he pulled out the pair with trains on them which made it far harder for me to argue against wearing them.

I'd initially protested, but Daddy told me they would be a constant reminder he was there for me. The training pants were snug and held my dick and balls firmly against my body. They were also much more modestly cut—and far thicker—than the underwear I normally wore. There was no mistaking these were made to hide any leaks a boy may have in his undies.

I really hoped I didn't test that during the interview.

The bright red waist and leg bands and the train going across the seat were vibrant and fun. The big train engine printed right over my dick made me laugh when I saw it the first time. Even taking into account the added bulk and the unfamiliar cut, I felt good in them. They did make me feel safe and protected, sort of like the diapers had. I wasn't ready to throw away my normal underwear for them, but the training pants had their own draws. Besides, I wasn't going to turn away anything that might help my stress levels.

By 7:45, the new management team was in my mom's kitchen peppering me with interview questions. Colt stood at my side, rubbing my back and letting me lean on him for support.

After the third time we'd gone over the questions about how long I'd known I was gay and how I'd met Colt—because he had to be Colt for the morning—I was starting to get frustrated.

"Guys, I've known I was gay for as long as I can remember. Us going over this question again and again isn't going to change it. I'm not going to alter my truth for anyone, especially the media," I finally snapped.

Harrison bumped my shoulder and gave me a nod of approval. He seemed almost as nervous as I was. Then again, he seemed to have a lot riding on me coming out.

Colt looked over at me. "You tell the truth. If you aren't comfortable with a question don't answer it, simple as that."

"Is Colt going to be part of the interview?" a red-headed guy from management asked us.

"I hadn't planned on it," I answered honestly.

"If it makes things easier for Derek, I'll do it. But this is about him coming out, not me."

The red head nodded, his heavy plastic glasses slipping slightly down his nose.

At 8:35, production vans showed up at the house and the living room began to transform in front of our eyes. My mom, for once, stepped back and let things happen without her input. Even my Dad and Jasper were in the house instead of outside with the animals. Neither could seem to make heads nor tails of the circus descending on the ranch.

"Derek, are you sure you're okay with this?" Jasper asked me quietly while temporary lighting was being erected across from the loveseat.

I nodded slowly. "I *was* sure about it until about five minutes ago. It seems... big."

Jasper nodded and glanced over at our dad. "He's worried about you."

I blinked. "What?"

"He's been at my house since 5:30 this morning. He's worried the media is going to eat you alive and your fans are going to turn their backs on you."

I was trying to parse out all the information Jasper was giving me. My dad hadn't spoken to me in months, but he was worried about me? Worried enough he was talking to Jasper about it, but he hadn't said anything to me. "Those things could happen. I'm really putting myself out there. But he doesn't need to worry about that, does he? It isn't his career or livelihood on the line today."

"Exactly. He can't do anything to protect you from whatever comes of this. The first week you were gone, he was a nervous wreck. He was concerned someone was going to find out you're gay. He still worries about what will happen if you come out. He's proud of you, Dare. He talks about how successful you are. He follows your career, you know? He just doesn't show it right."

My eyes filled with tears I didn't bother to hold in. I also didn't bother to keep my voice down when I practically yelled at Jasper. "It would have been nice for *him* to fucking tell me that! *He* hasn't spoken to me in months." I pointed to where my dad was standing and saw him flinch slightly. "No, I told him I was gay and he stopped talking to me. He sure has a funny way of showing he cares!"

Colt was at my side before I had the words out and pulled me into a tight embrace. I pushed my face into the side of his neck and took a few deep breaths trying to calm myself. The rest of the packed house was trying to ignore us as best they could.

"I'm sorry, I didn't mean to upset you," Jasper said from beside me.

By the time I looked up, my dad and Jasper were gone and my mom was standing next to Madeline looking worried. "Are you going to be okay?" he asked me, every bit of protective Daddy Dom evident in his voice.

I nodded slowly. "Sorry, what Jasper said just surprised me."

Colt pressed a gentle kiss to my forehead. "You've got this."

As he stepped away, the protective bubble he'd created dissolved and the chaos of the house came rushing back. I was instantly pulled in a number of different directions, including toward makeup which was now more important than ever. I hoped the makeup artist was good, because I could tell my eyes were going to look rough. They only had twenty minutes to work their magic because the interview had to happen so there was time for editing before it aired at eight that night.

I didn't have time to think about anything else until I finally sat down on the loveseat.

CHAPTER 38

COLT

As I'd held Derek in the middle of the living room while he tried to calm his stuttering breaths, all I could do was will myself not to have words with his dad. Brice had been cordial to me since I'd arrived, but had yet to say a thing to Derek. The entire house had heard Derek snap at his brother, but Brice had turned white and walked out before Derek had even stopped yelling.

When I was satisfied Derek was ready to face the room again, I kissed his forehead and stepped away. I watched as he got swept away by someone and turned to Madeline. "Where did Jasper and Brice go?"

She pointed out the back door. Well shit, there were 1500 acres of ranch out that door. They could be anywhere.

I stepped out of the house and didn't make it five feet before I heard a raised voice.

"What does he mean you haven't spoken to him since before he left?" Jasper was asking.

"I didn't know what to say!"

I stepped around the corner, pulling my coat around me to block some of the wind. "A great starting point would have been 'hello.' Or maybe, 'sorry,'" I interjected. I was pissed. I had to remember I was only Derek's boyfriend. While I was his Daddy, I wasn't his dad and I needed to not make things worse.

"He tells us he's gay and he leaves. What did he expect?" Brice demanded, but there was no bite to his words.

"He had obligations to fulfill. He *had* to leave. You're his dad, it was your job to tell him you don't hate who he is."

Brice's mouth opened and shut a number of times. "I-I don't hate him, I could never hate him."

Jasper looked as confused as I felt. "You sure have a strange way of showing that," I managed to say. "Coming out isn't easy, Brice. Ask anyone who's ever done it. We don't come out once, we come out over and over again. Derek thinks his own father hates him after coming out and yet he's willing to tell the world he's gay. He's prepared to lose his career over this."

Brice shook his head. "Colt, it's...it's not like that."

"Then tell me what it *is* like, because I don't understand."

Brice took a deep breath. "I'm scared."

"You're scared?" Jasper questioned, throwing his hands up in the air.

"I'm scared for him." Brice sighed. "He told us he's gay, and then he left on tour. It isn't like he's a pop music singer where they are singing about acceptance and performing at Pride. This is country music. A group of people who are driving around with Confederate flags on their trucks and spewing intolerance every chance they get. And my kid is out there with them! What happens now? Now he comes out and he's got a target on his back. What happens to his career? What happens to his life?"

I got it. Brice had gone about it all wrong, but he was scared and confused and he didn't know how to tell Derek. He probably felt like he should have the answers, but he didn't. The truth was, no one did.

"I'd always seen Derek falling in love with a woman and having the two point five kids, white picket fence life," Brice admitted. "Then he told us he's gay and that all changed. I thought he'd never find happiness with a man. He shows up here happier than I've ever seen him and I couldn't figure it out. Then my phone starts blowing up, people from church telling me he's been photographed kissing a guy. You show up a few hours later. It was confusing."

Confusing I could get. Not speaking to your son for months on end, I couldn't.

"As soon as I saw you two together, I knew you two were in love. And then all these preconceived notions I had about what his life was going to be like were changing. He looks at you like I still look at Marla, like you hung the moon. And you look at him like he's a precious gift."

My mouth hung open. Brice had just told me I loved Derek. Sure I had more intense feelings for him than I'd ever had for anyone else, but we hadn't even been together a full month and most of that had been long distance. *Was it possible to love someone after such a short period of time?*

Apparently, some of that thought was out loud.

"I fell in love with Marla on our first date," Brice admitted. "We were young, but I knew she was the one. It didn't even matter she'd been with my brother first. People want you to think it takes time to fall in love with someone, but sometimes, it just happens. You love my son and I see it in the way you look at him, the way you touch him. It's just taken me awhile to figure it all out. I don't hate him, or you."

I was doing a great impression of a fish at that point, my mouth opening and closing as I tried to figure out words. Thankfully, Jasper seemed to have enough words for me.

"Okay, first, eww, I didn't need to know about Mom and Uncle Joe, gross. Second, you should be telling this to Derek, not his boyfriend."

"I will," Brice promised. "Thank you for being there for Derek," Brice said to me.

"I'm always going to be there for Derek." I meant every word of it. I loved Derek so much my heart physically ached and I'd only figured out what that feeling was when Brice told me.

How did I miss that one?

CHAPTER 39

DEREK

THE INTERVIEW HAD GONE MUCH MORE SMOOTHLY than I'd expected. Simple questions about life on the road and being a relatively new band slowly morphed into harder questions about my personal life. Every time I got uncomfortable, I would glance up and see Daddy and Jasper and Harrison and my mom and, surprisingly, my dad watching me, giving me smiles and nods of encouragement.

Every time I felt myself getting nervous, I remembered the training pants Daddy had slipped on me after my shower. They hugged my waist and were snug around my balls. They were a constant reminder Daddy was there for me, making sure I had what I needed even if I couldn't physically touch him. The slightest shift in position was enough to remind me that, no matter how the day went, I would still have Daddy. He didn't care if I was a famous singer or not. I could be big or little. He wanted me any way he could have me and that was enough to help me through the stress and uncertainty of the interview.

When the interviewer finally got to the real reason we were sitting in my parents' living room on a Friday morning in February, I was feeling fairly confident.

"How has it been living your life in the public eye?" she asked me.

I chuckled. "It hasn't always been easy. I feel like my every move has been cataloged and not always for the best."

She nodded like it made perfect sense. "There were pictures a few days ago of you kissing someone who appeared to be a man at the Nashville airport. That had to be difficult."

"The person who snapped that picture caught me in an intimate moment with my boyfriend as I told him good-bye. If I had been kissing a woman, we wouldn't be here today."

"So, what you are saying is that those pictures were of you?"

I had to fight a groan. I hated the theatrical shit involved in this stuff. "Yes, there's no point in denying it. I am gay." I punctuated the last three words. "If I denied those pictures, there would eventually be more that surfaced. There would be rumors about why I never have a girlfriend with me at events. Honestly, I'd rather bring my boyfriend."

Her eyes widened slightly but she never missed a beat, "And how long have you known you're gay?"

I closed my eyes for a moment. I hoped it looked like I

was thinking, but in reality I was counting backward from ten so I didn't roll my eyes and ask her how long she knew she was straight. "When my older brother came home from first grade and announced he was going to marry the girl who sat next to him, I clearly remember telling him I was going to marry Harrison." I glanced over at Harrison and had to bite my cheek so I didn't laugh at his look of wide-eyed surprise.

"I didn't understand what it meant to be gay, I just knew I didn't want to marry a girl. My mom told me she didn't care who I married, but Jasper told me boys couldn't marry boys. Until a few years ago, he was technically right. I remember being confused, because I didn't want to marry a girl. From the look Jasper gave me that day, I knew I'd said something wrong, so I didn't tell anyone who I liked after that."

Jasper looked guilty. I didn't know if he remembered that conversation or not, but he had ducked his head and I could see the red on his cheeks.

"I grew up here in Oklahoma. My brothers and I were taught by the church that homosexuality is a sin. It took me until I was sixteen to be able to admit to myself that I'm gay. Within the last few years, I'd started accepting myself for the first time in my life and then my career took off. We shot to the top of the charts and I had to slip back into the closet. Hiding such an important part of my identity has been hard. So, while I'm not happy to have my personal business exposed so publicly, I'm glad I don't have to hide anymore."

After that, the interview wrapped up quickly. I was

anxious to get it over with once I'd finally admitted I was gay. I wanted to collapse into Daddy's arms and be done. Thankfully, before long, the interview was over and the crew was packing up in record time to make sure they had time to edit the footage.

The management team seemed to think I'd handled everything well enough because they were all smiles as they shook my hand and left the house. It seemed like, in the blink of an eye, the house had emptied out and Harrison was standing in the doorway saying goodbye to me.

"You wanted to marry me?" he snickered.

I shrugged. "I was six. You were my best friend. I haven't thought of you like that since we were little. I have my own man now anyway."

Harrison laughed. "Yeah, me too." It was out so quickly I almost thought I'd misheard him until he turned bright red. "Later, Dare." He was down the sidewalk and to his truck before I could respond.

Madeline left a few minutes later, thanking my mom profusely for the excessive amounts of food she had fed her that day and for the cookies Mom packed up. "You did well. I'm proud of you," Madeline said to me as she stood on her tiptoes to kiss my cheek.

The door shut and I sagged against it and closed my eyes, finally able to breathe for the first time since Madeline had shown up on our doorstep that morning.

"Dare, can I talk to you?" My dad's voice cut through my momentary relief. I cracked my eyes open to look at him and could see how uncomfortable he looked. I didn't know what to make of that. I looked over at Colt who was leaning against the counter, he gave me a hesitant nod, and I followed my dad around the corner and into his office.

I closed the door behind me in an effort to give us whatever privacy I could, I had no idea what was going to be said.

My dad leaned against his desk, hands gripping the wood surface as he braced himself. He was trying to look calm, but from the way his eyes darted around, I knew he was anything but. "I'm sorry."

My eyebrows shot up. "You're... what?" I shook my head and stared at him.

"When you came out to Mom and me, I was surprised. I never expected one of you boys to be gay. I-I had this very narrow view of what homosexuality meant for your life. I saw you spending your life alone, or if you came out, stuck here where you'd be judged for the rest of your life."

I furrowed my brows. What he was saying made no sense to me. "You stopped speaking to me because you didn't want me to be alone?"

"I was scared."

"Of me?"

Was he not making sense or was it just me?

"For you. I didn't want you to have a difficult life. I haven't known what to say to you. Then Colt shows up here this week and I've never seen you happier. Dare, he makes you happy."

"Um, yeah, he does." I couldn't keep the sarcasm out of my voice.

"I watched you guys dancing in the kitchen. You

looked exactly like your mom and me when we were first together. I watched him while you were doing the interview, there was nothing but love in his eyes. I'm pretty sure he would have traded places with you in a heartbeat if it would have made your life easier. I know I would have," he admitted quietly.

"He makes me happy," I said dumbly. I had no idea what else to say to him. I was on overload.

"He loves you. I see it in his eyes and in his interactions with you."

My eyes widened. "We've only been together a few weeks. I think it's too soon for that."

The smile my dad gave me was amused, "Do you really believe that? Or are you saying that because that's what you think is expected?"

I stopped myself before I could protest more. "I-I..."

Could I imagine my life without Colt—Daddy—in it?

I could easily see myself going home to him after a tour and curling up on the couch. Big or little, I wanted him in my life any way I could get him. That wobbly feeling I got in my stomach when I saw him and the that I felt when we parted ways, those feelings weren't love, were they?

I stood across from my dad for a moment, suddenly understanding what he was trying to explain to me.

"Holy shit," I said on an exhale. "I *do* love him."

My dad smirked. "That's what I thought." He sighed sadly. "Listen Dare, I'm sorry. I never meant to hurt you."

"Thank you, that means a lot to me."

It wasn't going to fix our relationship—not by a longshot—but it was a start. My dad was scared for me, and

CHAPTER 40

COLT

By the time we left for the guest house, Derek and I were both done. It had been a long and emotionally draining day. Neither of us had any desire to watch the interview. We'd lived it, we didn't need or want to see how it had been edited. It was out of our control how the world took it anyway and watching wouldn't help Derek.

If we stayed any longer, his entire family was going to know more about our relationship than either of us was comfortable with. Derek had called me Daddy three times between dinner and the time we left. The last time, I was pretty sure Marla had heard because we had become quite interesting to her those last few minutes.

"Can we watch cartoons tonight?" Derek questioned as we walked toward the guest house.

"I think that can be arranged."

"And diapers?" he asked bashfully.

"Of course. Let's get you inside. I'll start a fire to warm the living room up some."

Derek waited by the side of the bed for me to strip him out of his jeans and shirt. I took my time unbuttoning his flannel shirt and slipping it down his arms, then I slowly removed his jeans and underwear, depositing everything in the laundry pile in the corner of the room.

He flopped down on the bed and lifted his hips once I had the diaper under him. "Did you know there are groups that get together sometimes?" he mentioned.

The sentence probably wouldn't have made much sense to most people, but I knew he was talking about play-groups for littles.

I hadn't realized Derek had been researching age play until then. I wondered what else he'd found, but I nodded at his question. "Yes. Some littles have playdates and if they have Daddies or Mommies they go too."

"Have you ever been to one?" he asked as I dusted him with powder.

"Not to a dedicated playdate outside of a club scene. I've been involved in a few littles gatherings at clubs, though."

Derek was quiet for a few seconds. "Are they fun?" he asked as I secured each of the four tapes on his diaper.

I nodded slowly. "It is fun to see the littles getting to play and interact."

"I wish I could have a friend to play with," he admitted shyly. "I guess I'll just need to settle for oversharing with Ty."

My heart hurt for him. His personality was such that he would have a lot of fun playing with another little, but his job made it far too risky. I almost laughed because it would probably be easier if Derek were into puppy play, at least then he could have a mask. Instead, I squeezed his leg. "I think playdates would be hard for you, unfortunately."

Derek smiled at me. "It's okay, Daddy, I have a lot of fun with you." He sat up and let me guide his arms into a green pajama shirt with cars on it. Once it was pulled down, I guided his legs into the matching shorts and pulled them up.

The thick diaper under the thin cotton shorts was easily noticeable and made Derek waddle slightly as we headed toward the living room.

I moved the coffee table out of the way then went to the kitchen to make him a drink. I usually gave him sippy cups for playtime, but that night I poured juice into a bottle for him and capped it. I wanted him to be able to sink as far into his role as he wanted and I thought a bottle would help with that.

Once he was settled on the floor with his coloring books and bottle, I found some cartoons on the TV and set to work starting a fire. By the time the fire was crackling pleasantly in the fireplace, Derek's bottle was already gone. I was surprised at how fast he had drained the contents, though I probably shouldn't have been given how much he liked juice. I decided to refill his bottle with milk since he didn't need that much sugar before bed.

CHAPTER 41

DEREK

THE ADULT WORLD SLIPPED AWAY AS I WAS PLAYING. The interview didn't matter, nor did the next day—all that mattered was Daddy and my toys. And Daddy was taking care of everything. He was refilling my empty bottle and the fire was keeping the room warm. The world could have been coming down around me and I wouldn't have noticed.

By the time Daddy returned with a bottle of milk, I was lying on my stomach playing with my trains and the wooden train track after losing interest in my coloring book. I took it without thought and turned my attention back to my toys. I had no idea how much time had passed before my feet began to wiggle as I played. A few minutes later, my bladder felt full and my legs began to bounce. I had never worn a diaper long enough to end up with an uncomfortably full bladder and I didn't know what to do. Part of me wanted to continue playing with my trains, but another part of me wanted to ask to use the bathroom.

Was I allowed to use the bathroom when I was wearing a diaper?

Not knowing was frustrating and despite wanting to ask, the question seemed too daunting. I chose to take my blanket and crawl up onto the couch with Daddy and let him make the decision for me.

As I settled my body across his lap with my head on the arm of the couch, Daddy rubbed my lower belly. "I saw you doing a little dance on the floor. Do you need to go potty, buddy?"

I nodded nervously.

"Okay, you can stay here until you're wet and then we'll get you changed."

My eyes widened. I hadn't really thought much about *using* the diaper until that point. I wanted to argue and ask to use the bathroom, but I realized—with great relief— Daddy had made the decision already and it was out of my control. There was something freeing about knowing I didn't even have to worry about making it to the bathroom when I needed to go.

"It's okay, buddy," Daddy reassured me as he grabbed the remote for the TV and flicked through channels until he found my favorite cartoon. As we watched, he rubbed small circles on my stomach. I managed to completely forget about my bladder until the show was over and it had become an emergency.

"Daddy," I whimpered as my muscles clenched.

"Relax, we'll get you changed as soon as you're wet." With calm words and the gentle way he rubbed my stomach my bladder gave up the fight. Daddy kept rubbing my stomach lightly until my diaper was uncomfortably heavy and my bladder was shockingly empty.

"What a good boy," he praised when I was done. The praise caused me to blush, but I couldn't deny being happy I had made Daddy proud of me. "Let's go get you changed and we can come back out and clean up the toys before bed."

My thumb slipped into my mouth. I was laying on Daddy's lap in a heavy, wet diaper, and he was praising me. I couldn't seem to wrap my mind around what I had done before it occurred to me I didn't have to. It was Daddy's job to think and my job to feel. Right then, everything felt right. I was warm, Daddy was doting on me, and I felt loved. There wasn't a single thing about the situation I would change.

Daddy gave me a gentle push. "Let's go to the bedroom."

Reluctantly, I got up but nothing in me wanted to move until Daddy did. I had never felt this fuzzy before and yet, I didn't want to let the feeling go. When Daddy took my hand, I knew it was fine to follow and my feet started moving. My movements were awkward with the soaked diaper between my legs and he chuckled at my waddle.

"Up on the bed, buddy."

As I climbed up, I realized Daddy was treating this like it was something we'd done countless times before and the last few nerves I felt settled completely. I was Daddy's boy and I was happy with that.

He untaped the diaper and wiped my skin with a cool

wipe. I hadn't seen them in the room before, but it showed me how much thought he'd put into this moment. Knowing that using my diaper was something Daddy had planned and accounted for, but had never pushed me to do made the moment even more special.

Part of me worried that once I was changed, the feeling would end and I wasn't ready to go back to being grown-up Derek yet. Before I was ready, I was in a dry diaper and Daddy had my pants pulled back up. I braced myself for things to change, but when he held out his hand the same gentle smile was on his face. "You need to clean up your toys and while you do that, I'll make you a bottle."

I smiled and took his hand. "Milk, Daddy?"

"You bet. But you can't have it until you clean up all of your toys."

I nodded and followed him back to the living room where he left me to clean up. Even though every one of my trains was out of the bin, it only took a few minutes to put them away. It would have gone even faster if I'd removed my thumb from my mouth, but it was too tempting, so I cleaned up one-handed. Daddy was already on the couch when I was done cleaning up.

"Thank you for cleaning up so nicely," he told me as I headed over to him. I loved that I was able to sit on Daddy's lap without feeling like I would crush him. It felt natural to settle over him so my head was resting on his shoulder and my legs were over his lap. Opening my mouth for my bottle was as natural as parting my lips for my thumb. With Daddy holding the bottle for me, I just got to relax and soak up all the attention he was giving me.

We were quiet while I had my bottle, but Daddy trailed light touches up my arm and across my shoulders and back down, soothing me into a place where I was only half awake. When I sucked air instead of milk, Daddy pulled the nipple from my mouth.

"I love you," I said and my eyes widened. I did love him, and I knew it, but was it absurd to say it right then? Would he believe I meant it as both little Derek and big Derek?

I didn't have to worry long because he placed his lips to my forehead then pulled back. "I love you, too, Derek. Little or big, I love you."

I hummed my appreciation and let my eyes flutter shut. It was then that I fully understood I would always be at home with him. I had, quite literally, run right into the man of my dreams and there was no way I was going to give him up now that I had him.

EPILOGUE

Derek

I placed my guitar case beside the boxes lining the wall in the spare room at Daddy's house—*our* house. Ten months on tour with Hometown, over 125 shows played, and I was finally home. He'd asked me to move in with him the last time he flew out to spend a long weekend with me. It had only gotten harder and harder to be away from him as the tour progressed, so moving in together seemed like the next logical step.

The band would be in Nashville for the rest of the summer because we had the Christmas album to work on. Leslie hadn't been happy with me for weeks after the meeting in Nashville. It took him almost a month to secure the rights to "At Home." The original band had been leery about us covering it. It ended up taking a phone call from

Harrison, Gina, and me where we explained that it meant a lot to us because we had listened to it so frequently over the holidays.

We may have left out the fact that everyone else in the band had been ready to kill me for most of December.

I planned on writing a dedication to Colt for the sleeve of the printed album. The song meant even more to me now that I had a place to come home to. For the first time in my adult life, I felt at home. It was because I knew I had my boyfriend—*my Daddy*—waiting for me. He was there to catch me when I fell and celebrate my successes. I wouldn't have survived the second half of the tour without his support and I couldn't imagine my life without him in it.

We had all held our ground about not extending the tour and I couldn't have been happier with the decision. Daddy and I had flown directly to Oklahoma from the last tour stop in Seattle so we could pack up my belongings and drive my truck to Tennessee. Since I'd never lived alone, I didn't have much aside from clothing and a few boxes of personal stuff, so everything fit nicely in the bed of my truck.

Looking back on where I was in February, my life was different in almost every way. Coming out hadn't been the downfall of Hometown. Yes, there were a number of haters and hashtags like #BoycottHometown and #DereksGay even trended on social media for a few days. But the dreaded album sales slump never happened. Actually, we had seen a steady increase in album and ticket sales since the interview aired.

My inbox had been flooded with letters from people across the world thanking me for coming out and telling me how much it meant to them. The letters of support far exceeded the small number of emails telling me I was going to hell.

The best part of coming out was that Colt was able to come to events with me. He always seemed to be willing to take a day or two off to make sure he could be there. The first few events were difficult on both of us as we were hounded for information about our relationship, but by April there was another celebrity who had grabbed the attention of the media. In a world filled with rich and famous people doing absurd things, I was boring. The celebrity gossip world was filled with people far more fascinating than me. It was only a matter of time before someone did something more outlandish than coming out as gay. Even if I found myself on the front pages of magazines for a few weeks, it was just a waiting game before someone else became tabloid fodder.

I unlocked my phone and opened the group text with my family that had been in use almost constantly since I left Oklahoma in February.

Me: *At home. Made it safe.*

Mom: *Oh good, I was starting to worry.*

Jasper: *Don't listen to her, she was only worried you would call and say you were coming back. She already has plans for your room.*

Me: *LMAO! At least let my sheets cool off before you take over my bedroom!*

Ty: *The hazmat team I hired can't be here to sanitize* *your sex palace for another three days. The sheets will be cold by then.*

Jasper*: Ugh, don't want to think about what'll be growing on them by then...*

Me*: We were in the house! It wasn't like we had wild sex!*

Ty*: Huh, could have fooled me with those noises coming from your room last night!*

Jasper*: TMI TMI TMI!*

Mom*: Glad our room is downstairs.*

Dad*: Enough already, some of us are trying to work. The constant dinging is driving the horses crazy.*

Dad*: Glad you made it to TN alright.*

Me*: You guys are sick, sick people. Talk with you all soon. Ty, tell Dec that we're thinking of him and hope he gets through basic okay.*

I smiled and went to find Daddy. I was ready to relax for the rest of the evening. I felt the training pants he put me in before we left Oklahoma hugging me tightly as I headed out of the room. Walking toward my room, I had a little bounce in my step. I was home and soon I'd be playing in the living room in a thick diaper. Daddy was already there with a diaper and pajamas laid out for me and my blanket laying on my pillow.

I couldn't help a smile from spreading across my face as I climbed onto the bed. Knowing I was at home with an amazing boyfriend, and Daddy, at my side now, I was prepared to face whatever was thrown my way... after playtime.

Not ready to leave Pleasant? Check out these books

CATCH UP with Derek and Colt on their first Valentine's Day, in this sweet and very sexy Valentine's Novella, *Be My Home*.

WANT to learn how Ty and Declan find their happily ever after? Find *Coming Home* here. The second installment of Finding Home is sure to bring laughs and sexy fun as the two find happiness away from Oklahoma. Also available on Audible.

FIND OUT MORE ABOUT JASPER, Harrison, and Greg—the man that steals their hearts—in the third and forth books of the Finding Home series, *Close to Home* and *Already Home*. It doesn't matter how close or far from the ranch these guys are, home will always be where the heart is. Also available on Audible *Close to Home* & *Already Home*.

. . .

AND A LONGER FOLLOW-UP with *all* the Finding Home characters can be found in *Home for Christmas*. Make sure to pick it up today!

DEREK AND COLT might have been my first MCs, but the two have never left my world. They are now living in Middle Tennessee and show up randomly in many of my books. If you want to keep following their lives, make sure to catch up with them:

Curiosity
Attraction
Zander
Sunshine Sky

Thank You

Dear Reader,

Thank you for reading *At Home*! I hope you enjoyed reading about Derek and Colt as much as I enjoyed writing about them. Derek is a chatterbox and has convinced me that his story is not finished yet. He and Colt will return in Ty and Declan's story, *Coming Home*, due out early 2019.

This book would never have been possible without the support of my family and friends who kept me going when I thought it was impossible. I'll be forever grateful for my beta readers, editor, and friends—both old and new—who pulled together to make this dream a reality.

Please consider leaving a review to help others find my books.

With Love,

ABOUT THE AUTHOR

Carly Marie has had stories, characters, and plots bouncing around her head as long as she can remember. She began writing in high school and found it so cathartic that she's made time for it ever since. With the discovery of m/m romance, Carly knew she'd found her home. She was surprised to learn not everyone has sexy characters in their head, begging for their stories to be written. With that knowledge, a little push from her husband, and a lot of encouragement from newfound friends, she jumped into the world of publishing.

Carly lives in Ohio with her husband, four girls, two cats, and 14 chickens. The numerous plot bunnies running through her head on a daily basis ensures that she will continue to write and share stories.

Connect with Carly!

Facebook: facebook.com/groups/CarlyMarie/

Instagram: instagram.com/carlymariewrites

Goodreads: goodreads.com/CarlyMarieWrites

Made in the USA
Columbia, SC
10 March 2022

57510733R00190